Happiness

Is Just
A Pill
Away

DAVID GRAD

Tellwell Talent
www.tellwell.ca

ISBN
978-1-77370-345-9 (Paperback)
978-1-77370-346-6 (eBook)

To my friends and family,
Despite my often aloof and eccentric behaviour, you are always there
for me. I don't say thank you very well, so allow me to type it.
Thank you for the support, friendship, and belief
you've given me throughout my life.

This story has been helped along by three wonderful people:

Stephanie Loewen
Ron Ernst
Sean Devine

Stephanie, the detailed feedback and insight you provided on the rough-est of first drafts shaped the central character and guided the story.
Thank you!

Ron, the world's greatest roommate (from my perspective at least), you used to tease me for working too hard. Your clever rhyme, Dave the Slave, was a call to not let work get in the way of life. I dedicate the character of Dave the Slave to your rhythmic taunts.

Sean, thank you for the Devine intervention and support through the final edits. Your thoughts, critique, and feedback improved the novel (especially the ending!) and left me feeling more comfortable with the final story.

Given the opportunity, people will surprise you with acts of generosity and kindness. This book is dedicated to all those who supported the publication of this story, for your contributions have made this possible.

To my Nana and Scrabble Master, Irene Kucenty, thank you for being my biggest fan.

Andrea Scocchia

Andrew Bettencourt

Bob and Hanusia Tkaczyk

Chris Thiessen

Dawna Wojkowski

Darren Sancartier

David Grad Sr.

Elizabeth Brooker

Glen Fenwick

Hanna Sieben

Jared Hagens

Joe Kelly

Judy Grad

Julian Diaz-Abele

Kathy Niziol

Kevin Oliver

Laura McKenzie

Lauren Whittaker

Lindsay Grad

Lynn Wood

Mark O'Riley

Mark Symeonakis

Melani Decelles

Michael A. Kandrack

Michael Cechovsky

Nikolai Stefan Tkaczyk III

Rob Mausser

Rosemarie and Alex North

Sanjana Vijayann

Sean Lund

Sean and Sara McFarlane

Sonya Penner

Steve Tremblay

Susie Taylor

Trevor Cava

Tracy Foster

Trevor Sowinski

Valerie Williams

Wayne Burr

"One of the great paradoxes of life is that self-awareness breeds anxiety."
– Irvin D. Yalom, *Love's Executioner*

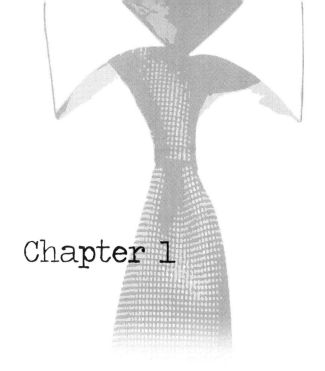

Chapter 1

I should consider myself fortunate. Five days a week I drive alongside the sun as it rises from its slumber, stretching across the horizon in fiery tones of red, orange, and yellow. Serenity lies just outside my driver side window. All I have to do is turn my head. Instead, I'm fixated on the road and rear fender scudding along the pavement in concert with me. There may have been a time I looked out the window with curiosity, but routine has no time for curiosity. Lately, I've struggled to shake the feeling that routine is just a strategy to avoid thinking about what I'm missing. At work I find myself imagining what it's like outside. I picture myself sitting in the sun doing nothing but looking around at the world, enjoying the opportunity to sit unmolested by responsibility and routine. Smiling.

But thoughts of unattainable freedom always fade to regret.

On cue, my mind pulls me from the imaginary park bench to stand before an internal crowd of criticism and account for the ongoing streak of missed opportunities. Routine drives back the mass of self-conscious objectors into silence. Check email. Update task list. Don't think about how I could be sitting outside in the sun. Settle for the lukewarm glow of phosphor caused by excited low-pressure mercury-vapour gas. My sun is a long, thin, and cloudy glass tube directly above my head.

People weren't meant to cultivate under the warm glow of a fluorescent tube. Sometimes I wonder if fluorescent lights were designed to suppress our drive by enveloping us in the rapture of complacency. The constant hum lulls us into believing we don't need anything more from life than a steady job and the newest cell phone. Our day is accompanied by this subtle song hidden in the white noise of our reverberating environment, drowning out thought with something more repetitive. *Work. Work. Work. Work. Work. Work. Work.*

Daily routine diverts my dissatisfaction.

So here I sit, Monday to Friday, in the same leatherette chair. Leather is too grand an expense for the regular workforce; simulated leather provides all the thrill for a fraction of the price. Leatherette also doesn't require animal sacrifice to provide comfort, so I rest easy knowing that blood was not shed for my vanity. I work in the standard office setting that you would see in any television show or magazine. Grey tone, symmetry, and portable walls. Pictures cut out of magazines surround me in half-hazard protest against symmetry and order. Pictures cut from travel and nature magazines are portals into other worlds, fueling fantasies about being surrounded by lakes, mountains, trees, and open space. About being someone who breathes easy and lives by their own schedule. I can't seem to find any satisfaction in the present from what is unfolding in front of me. Are the people around me OK with this? I can't be alone.

To soothe my nerves I use a pen to tap a busy beat on my desk and gaze into a picture of a long, winding rural road. There's a single car disappearing into the horizon and I'd give anything to be sitting in it right now. As I shrink from the world in my office chair, a shrill … cackle drags me back. On the other side of my cubicle wall, coworkers have managed to yank me from my scenic drive with their overenthusiastic chatter. Managing my distaste for small talk is an ongoing project. The thought of it churns my insides. For whatever reason, the world seems to cherish short, meaningless, and forgettable spurts of conversation. Small talk is nothing more than a public masturbation session. People keep trying to get off all over me, but I don't want any part of the conversational circle jerk.

I often wonder if people notice the invisible knife twisting its way through my gut when they talk to me. I try to survive the benign chore of small talk, but it gets harder every day. People constantly try to use me as a willing partner to get themselves off conversationally. I feel it is a sort of molestation, being forced to sit through unsolicited and unwanted small talk. Meaningless words and phrases grope me, satisfying the needs of the speaker at my expense.

"I think I'll go to my cottage this weekend," moans one man.

Terrific.

"I started a new diet. Works great," a woman exclaims in ecstasy.

Good for you.

Man licks lips slowly, "You catch that game last night?"

What a doozy.

"It's too hot outside."

Uh huh.

"It's too cold outside."

If only it were hot outside …

About to reach climax, a man shouts wildly, "You know what the problem with our filing system is?"

I'm going to shove your head up your ass and make you taste how full of shit you are. I wonder for a moment if I said that out loud. Nothing. He keeps talking. I guess not.

I just nod my head and affirm Jim of his opinion. Once he has reached his conversational climax, he celebrates by taking a large bite out of a donut, away from me. It's about time. I look down at my desk and the mountain of paperwork that lies before me and feel nothing. Despite the pending deadlines and never-ending supply of new assignments, I never seem to care. Not a single drop of panic sets in. It's hard to care about your job when you know your job couldn't care less about you. Where's the reciprocity? I like getting paid. I enjoy the lifestyle I've become accustomed to over the past five years through my employment. I relish the comforting feeling provided by each paycheque deposited directly into my bank account every other Friday, and that comfort is sufficient motivation to work just enough to not get noticed.

Anyway, I think the people I work with panic more than enough for me to afford the ability to be apathetic about my job performance. The room is so thick with panic I could slice it with a knife and serve it with a morning tea. My coworkers' panic is not just a noticeable feeling in the air; it's also a noticeable addition to the background noise of the lights. The pitter-patter of pens, toes, and fingertips. Nervous ticks of the perpetually anxious. People made anxious by the constant fear of being caught doing what they're not supposed to be doing.

Looking for funny pictures on the internet.

Texting.

Taking an extra thirty minutes at lunch.

Looking up postings of better jobs.

Daydreaming.

Part of me thinks that dreaming is the point of life – why else would we have such vivid and satisfying imaginations? People with overactive imaginations are chastised for not focusing on the here and now, but I think that the punishers of dreamers must suffer from underactive imaginations. Why would I ever want to spend my entire day conscious and in the present? What does my life offer me to enjoy and feel exhilarated by right now, in this moment? Email, paperwork, and interactions with my coworkers not only constitute the overwhelming majority of my day, but they also happen to be my three most hated activities in life. We all want a vacation away from our lives, and dreaming is the only way most of us can afford to get away from it all.

When I need a break from the minutia, I grab a folder, put some papers in it, and hold a pen. People recognize you mean business when your hands are full of office supplies. Office supplies can help create the successful illusion that you're in transit to or from a meeting, thereby affording you a few minutes of peace. It doesn't matter whether you're coming or going, because you're in that precious transitory moment in between tasks. Avoiding any social transaction that might take place while traveling the *in-between* is understandably necessary when you're busy.

To avoid conversation you have to dress up more than your outward appearance. A folder is only a prop, and a prop is only as good as the actor who holds it. People see an appropriate office artifact, and they are only half sold on the idea that you are too busy to talk. Since a folder is not out of place, you need to sell the idea of being too busy to talk with your eyes and the pace of your feet.

The eyes can speak volumes about you, although this is a concept that has not caught on with the majority of the human race. People tend to fixate on the lips and their constant flubbing about. What lips are able to express can be summed up in a matter of moments with the slightest nuance of the eyes; you just have to know how to give it. A coordinated gesture of the eyes is like sending a telepathic message to inform the subconscious of the person opposite you.

So here I go. 10:15 am. My watch reassures me that the morning is passing as slowly and painfully as I had thought.

Why can't I win the lottery?

Deep breath in. Deeper breath out. I grab the brown legal size file folder from under the unkempt paper organizer that taunts me daily. To make the file folder look more impressive I stuff whatever papers I can find into it. This isn't enough, I think to myself.

I sink deep into my chair. My hands cover my face as my elbows keep my head from its eventual freefall into the edge of my desk. My shirt sticks to my skin from nervous perspiration. Thinking about having to endure more small talk is making my stomach churn and heart run wild.

Inspiration strikes hard and often without notice. From between the cracks of my fingers I notice a box on the floor.

This is it.

No one would question a man with a box in his hands.

Just when your belief in God begins to falter, a small insignificant miracle appears before your eyes and reaffirms your belief. Of course, if you stopped to consider that this so-called *God* put you in the predicament you are currently facing, you might question the need for a miracle. I can only assume that these small insignificant miracles are less a means by which divine intervention seeks to provide us with a remarkable moment of hope than they are the byproduct of our own thoughts. If God did indeed grant humans free will, then he most certainly wouldn't use divine intervention to rob us of the freedom to feel miserable. God certainly wouldn't make our lives easier because we asked nicely through prayer. He is not a genie here to grant our wishes: life is tough because we make it tough. We want it tough. Otherwise, what would we complain about at parties?

Science is much simpler for the mind to understand. It provides the comfort of rules and predictable behaviours, leaving little to belief. Science has conspired to put this box in front of me, and I intend to make the best of it. So I pry my hands out from under my face, adjust my shirt, stand up tall, and canvas the room, not that there's anyone in particular I am trying to avoid. My contempt for people doesn't discriminate. My hatred is an equal opportunity employer. I map out the least populated route from my desk to the farthest stairwell exit so I can make a quiet getaway.

With the box in my hand I start the show. Turn on a smile, initiate squint, follow invisible tennis match with eyes, and increase the pace of my feet to create a panicked frenzy that reverberates off the carpet. My feet take me past Linda's desk first.

Linda recently got divorced and I can smell the desperation in the air. Linda needs a distraction from the ultimate truth she has recently uncovered.

Love will fail us all.

Love is most likely something that Shakespeare made up. I'd like to read a realistic love story where two people fall madly in love within minutes of meeting each other for the first time. For the guy, it is the most attractive girl who shows any interest in him. The guy feels confident that this girl may even consider having sex with him on a regular basis. For the girl, it is the most attractive guy who is confident enough to say something interesting to her. She finds his physical appearance to be agreeable. After scanning the room, she believes this man is likely the best looking option available to her. The girl uses his looks to rationalize that he is likely everything she wants in a man: sensitive, but tough; ambitious, but not a workaholic; extremely confident, but not cocky; honest, but not too honest; and charming, but only to her. Influenced by internal dialogue with his libido, the man rationalizes that he should agree to be whoever she wants him to be. Our two lovebirds spend many months courting each other by pretending to share the same interests. After many expensive dinners and signing up for fitness classes, they decide to move in with each other and take their loving relationship to another level. From the moment they start unpacking the boxes in their new apartment they start bickering about which closet is best for linen, what cupboards the plates and cups should be placed in, and how to decorate the living room. Within weeks, bickering blossoms into passionate yelling about each other's faults. Long periods of silent treatment are enforced because someone didn't show their appreciation for a home-cooked meal. The shower becomes clogged with hair. Soon the little things they hate about each other outnumber the things they love about each other. The only way they survive the relationship is by accepting the fact that they have to endure everything they hate about the other person. Love the way it is written and portrayed in film doesn't exist because it ignores effort. The Greeks used two masks to represent drama: one crying mask, and one laughing mask. Love should be represented by two masks as well: one angry, and one happy. Love and hate can't exist without each other. I'd explain all this to Linda, but I've already walked past her. I can't seem to care about the problems of others, so Linda will have to learn to accept on her own the inseparable nature of love and hate.

Oh my god.

I stop dead and close my eyes. I hate my coworkers, so does that mean I love them? *No.* I shake my head and continue to walk. To love something is to accept everything about it you hate. To hate something is to understand there is nothing about it you love. I hate my colleagues because I love nothing about them.

These are deep thoughts to have in the morning. Must be from all the walking I am doing. I make my way past Steve. Steve is a complete asshole. Steve is compelled to exclaim his triumphs over women like Linda in detail – perfectly nice girls who just wanted someone to look at them with sincere lust. Too bad these women can't tell the difference between the lust for an opportunity to get themselves off on a girl that looks *'easy'*, and the lust to better someone's life.

Steve's an asshole and love will always fail Linda because the ultimate truth is that deep down inside, we all just want to service ourselves.

Right now, I am servicing myself by ignoring Steve. Our eyes meet briefly as I walk by his desk. I can see him purse his lips. His body opens up, he lifts his arms from his desk, and his mouth just about forms a sound when I suddenly and abruptly cut him off in the act.

"Can't talk," I blurt out. From the corner of my eye I see Steve sit back down. I can't see the disappointment on his face because I've already walked past him. Too bad.

I keep walking towards the stairwell. The carpet absorbs the impact of my feet as I quicken my pace. In America, people do whatever they can to avoid any sort of physical labour. They certainly don't want to deal with the laborious task of walking up and down stairs during work hours. Imagine the perspiration people would have to endure if they took the stairs. It's a daily struggle for most Americans to avoid the uncomfortable feeling of sweat on the forehead or the awkward tickle of sweat beading down the back. So the stairwell has become a refuge for lost souls and people who want to avoid socializing with other human beings. The stairwell is my fortress of solitude.

I can see the door now. It's only fifteen feet away. Maybe twenty. I've waded my way through a maze of cubicles, and like any good maze I have had to avoid its randomly placed traps, dead ends, and possibilities.

You really have to map out where you're going in life.

My path takes me to the outermost edge of my office. I see everything from here. The dismal grey carpeting growing like algae on our perfectly placed cubicle walls, accented perfectly by the slightly lighter grey paint covering the barren office walls. Directly across from me is the hub of the office: *the staff coffee maker.* This is where the worker drones like to buzz about aimlessly, sucking back their government regulated drug.

Caffeine.

Caffeine is another tool used to ensure complacency. Every magician knows for a trick to be successful you need a distraction. Well, the best trick ever pulled off en masse was convincing the cackle of people that comprise the bulk of this planet that they're OK with their shitty lives. The dependency created by caffeine and sugar has created the perfect distraction from any real problems in life. Instead of engaging in the pursuit of happiness, people are too drowsy, high-strung, or desperate for their next fix to realize that their lives are trite and meaningless. They are also duped into spending $4.80 on a grande with whipped topping and a sprinkle of cinnamon. Of course, I think this behavior can also be equated to the general stupidity of the average person. The more the human race procreates, the greater the disparity between smart and dumb grows. Unfortunately, the dumbest end of the gene pool seems to be getting more crowded as of late.

I'm almost at the stairwell. My eyes are trying their best to look distressed, like I have a deadline to keep. I've got the box gripped tightly in my hands and my body looks as unapproachable as I can make it. My shoulders are tight and I've clenched my sphincter real tight. I figure I might as well give it a hundred and ten percent.

Three cubicles to go.

I walk past Mary. Mary is bland. Her complexion is lacklustre, her hair is dull, and her clothing choices are always safe. She wears nothing but solid colours and strictly avoids wearing anything bright. Her broad shoulders are perhaps her most attractive feature. Her waist seems slim, and her posture is pretty average. I've never actually noticed Mary stand up before and so I find myself wondering about her butt, specifically the shape of it. Is it round?

Flat? Odd ... I've never been more attracted to Mary than right now as I pass her desk and ponder the possibilities of her butt.

Maybe she has no legs. That does it. Just like a cold shower, I am instantly turned off.

Two cubicles remain.

I see Dave hard at work typing his life away. Dave the Slave is a model employee, typical nerd, and my pick for office serial killer. Dave hides his intentions in a way that makes him an impossible guy to read. I'm never able tell what he is thinking, so I imagine he is thinking a lot about something terrible. I've read about something called a genuine smile, which is exactly what it sounds like. Dave smiles an awful lot. He smiles about sitting alone at lunch. He smiles about the excessive workload piled on him by his boss and coworkers. He smiles when other people treat him like dirt. He even smiles when congratulating all those undeserving people who get promoted over him. I don't see a genuine smile when I watch Dave curl his lips and raise his eyebrows. I see a practiced, dishonest smile. I see a layer of protective armour that keeps people from knowing how terrible he actually feels.

One cubicle remains between me and the stairwell. Jeff casually lunges out of his dwelling and moves instantly into an uncomfortable lean at the side of his cubicle, as if it were mere happenstance that he is about to cut me off. I try to keep pace and sidestep past him. My neck strains as the inexplicable urge to make eye contact and nod my head takes hold.

I look directly into Jeff's eyes.

Don't do it, Jeff. Don't do it. Just nod and mind your own business. Jeff forms half a smile and inflates his chest as he takes a deep breath and exhales.

"Couple of us are going out for –"

"Sorry," I cut Jeff off. "Can't talk. Got this box." Motioning my eyes towards the box, I lift it up in an apologetic gesture.

"What about the box?" Jeff's lips curve into an unmistakable smirk.

Checkmate. "The box ... I am delivering it ... to ... I am delivering it."

"I see. Well anyway, a bunch of us are grabbing some beers tonight. You want to join us?"

At first I'm astonished at Jeff's ability to completely ignore the fact that I am holding a box, but that astonishment is quickly overshadowed by the disbelief that I am actually invited out somewhere. No, I think to myself. But my lips never get the memo.

"Great. O'Flaherty's pub at nine. Gonna get real drunk." Jeff points at me. I'm not sure what the purpose of him pointing at me at this juncture in the conversation is, but here it is. Jeff's arm is floating in the air and his index finger is pointed at my chest.

"Mary is coming."

That legless whore. "Mary? Sounds good. I'll be there."

I walk into the stairwell with the box still in my hands. It's cold, but clean. Not many feet find their way to these steps. It's like no one even knows the stairs exist as an option for moving between floors. No more than a few seconds pass before I throw the box down the stairs and hunker down on a step in a sulk.

If I throw myself down these stairs hard enough, I can put an end to it all. Or maybe I would just end up a vegetable. At least I wouldn't have to go to work. Or get jerked off on at O'Flaherty's tonight.

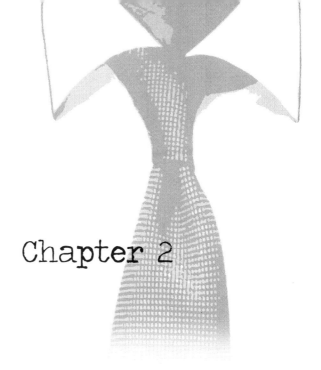

Chapter 2

8:00 pm. Getting ready for a casual time out on the town. In the town. On the town. I can't seem to remember what the actual saying is. Shrugging my shoulders, I focus on the usual assortment of cleansing tasks necessary before I feel comfortable enough to force myself into a social situation. A shower is a must, mostly to wash away the sweat that has accumulated in my underwear all day. Long periods of sitting tend to have that effect on me. It reminds me of the puddle of sweat toast leaves on a plate if left sitting too long.

I feel sick thinking about this morning. Why did I say yes? It was a knee-jerk reaction. "YES" just blurted out, as if I was flinching because some strange object had come screeching out across the room at me. My only option was to throw my hands up in terror and scream "yes!" Has evolution resulted in our fight or flight system instinctively responding to social calls to protect ourselves from being hated by others?

8:20 pm. I've finished grooming my body and draped myself in the appropriate garb. A pair of fitted jeans that say I'm comfortable and relaxed, yet fitted enough to show off my incredibly average physique. I don't want to seem too dressy, so I avoid any polos or crisp dress shirts. Instead, I slip on a wrinkled, plaid button-up.

Which begs the question: Why do I care? I never thought I was the kind of person who cared what others think, but I suppose it can't hurt to have the people admire your choice in attire.

8:30 pm. I'm out the door and walking the six blocks to O'Flaherty's. I figure I will arrive modestly late to show how cavalier I am about the whole situation. I want everyone to think that I had shit to do and better places to be. Of course I don't have anywhere else to be, but everyone pretends to be something they aren't. Interacting with others is just a game of pretend.

The sidewalk is littered with people turned inward in their collective entrancement by cellphones. No mucking about with civility, they are driven to get wherever they are going. If you look into the eye of a street urchin, you find a glassy stare looking right through you. You don't even get the courtesy of an icy stare that would make you feel like you might have something in your teeth, for that would require acknowledgment that you exist. People are suffering from an oversaturation of lost souls on the sidewalk, travelling the miles between where they came from and where they're going. The only way to keep sane in a world where you are perpetually walking by people you will never get the chance to know or have any sort of meaningful interaction with is to simply look past them. Strangers can't exist if you don't acknowledge them. Self-preservation is isolation.

Four blocks from the pub now.

The good thing about walking at night is the cool breeze keeping my armpits from developing unsightly stains. I'm irritated about having to meet my co-workers at the pub, but after several blocks I am feeling invigorated. There must be something about fresh air and exercise that is changing my state of mind. Or maybe it's the new surroundings, the thought of entering a new situation that isn't the predictable reality of my usual Monday to Friday. I'm breaking through the fog of routine and real close to not being an asshole. I wonder how long this will last.

Two blocks away from the pub now.

A man shoulders me as he walks by. He doesn't apologize and he doesn't look up from his phone. He simply doesn't care that he has caused an interruption in my life. He is the third person in the last fifteen minutes to shoulder me without so much as a hint of concern. No one gets out of the fucking way. It's always up to me to move. These zombies clomping around the streets never seem to bump into each other, but as soon as I throw myself into the mix, everyone is walking into me. Am I out of sync? Am I invisible? I wish. If I were invisible I would slap the phones right out of people's hands and force strangers to stand and stare at each other until one of them flinched and said *hello*. These people have convinced themselves that no one else on this sidewalk exists, that no one else on their path matters. The world is asshole-centric, so why shouldn't I be the one to move out of *their* way. It's surprising that I've never seen anyone walk into someone else on the street. Egos colliding as each person refuses to acknowledge the presence of someone else on the path they chose to venture. If two people were to walk into each other, would they then take a few minutes to talk to each other? Or would they just grunt angrily and continue on their way?

One block away from the pub.

What does Mary's butt look like? I wonder this, and I'm suddenly and inappropriately jarred from my spell of anger by the thought of asses. Maybe this will be the night I see what her butt looks like. I come to the stark realization that if Mary's butt doesn't meet or exceed the standards set by my imagination, I will be severely disappointed, so much so that I risk tonight being a total disappointment all based on the curves Mary's DNA has provided her.

I never imagined that someone's buttocks could have such an emotional effect on me.

At the door. I can see my reflection glistening in the parts of the gold door handle that aren't covered by disgusting hand-stains. It seems appropriate that I accessorize myself with a smile before opening the door, since no one likes a grumpy Gus.

Smile. Open door.

Instantly I see my welcoming committee seated right next to the bar. Well done, Jeff. Apparently I am not the only one who has to drown my personality in alcohol for other people to like me. Or maybe they have to use alcohol to drown out each other's personalities to get through the night. Either way, I decide I am going to have a drink or five.

In one smooth fluid motion, Jeff slithers out of his seat and extend his hand. "Hey! Glad to see you made it out." Steve remains seated, but gives me the wink and the gun before focusing his attention on the girls seated across from him. He seems to be wearing the same shirt as Jeff, only in a different colour.

"Wouldn't miss it," I manage to blurt out with a forced grin. I look over at Mary, give her my best smile, and half hope she stands up so I can finally see what her lower body looks like.

"Mary, how's it going?" She remains seated and has what looks like a sweater tied around her waist. Has that trend made it full circle?

Why I bothered asking her how "it" is going is beyond me, but I've now provided her with an opportunity to detail her entire day. I don't just mean a few details about her afternoon, it's been about seven minutes and she is still recounting her day. Apparently, "it" is a loaded concept, consisting of a detailed account of her daily interactions and accomplishments. I continue grinning and nodding my head in affirmation of Mary's every word. She must realize I don't care, but she continues to look for her conversational climax. Finally she stops. She must have gotten off.

About time. I hope she doesn't like to cuddle after.

I close my eyes tight and try to imagine myself having fun. Maybe if I can imagine it, I can will it to come true. In the split second that my eyes are closed I manage to work out how much effort I am going to have to put forth pretending to enjoy being at the pub. I manage to catch a glimpse of myself dancing awkwardly with Mary, her sweater draped like a cape from her waist fluttering with every gyration.

The façade of sociability is a strenuous task.

"What was that all about?" Mary imitates me by closing her eyes and pretending to be woken up from a deep sleep. Jeff and Steve share a laugh at my expense.

"Are we that boring? Come on man, liven up. Have a drink." Jeff pours a glass of beer from the pitcher on the table and pushes it towards me.

"Would you look at those girls? They're just waiting for some guy to come talk to them." Steve looks like a kid on Christmas morning: his eyes are wide and he is too excited to sit still. "Who's going to come with me? I can't go by myself."

Jeff looks over at me, "Well, he can't go. He hasn't even touched his drink yet. I guess that leaves it up to me. I'll have to do the responsible thing and go with Steve to talk to those two beautiful women." Jeff tips back the rest of his drink and playfully grasps Steve's shoulders as they both leave our table.

It's now just Mary, myself, and beer at our table. Far too little beer for my comfort, so when a waitress walks by I wave my hand in panic. Please rescue me and bring more beer.

"Another pitcher please, and can I get a rum and Coke?" The waitress nods and looks over at Mary.

"Can I get a Long Island Iced Tea?"

"Put that on my tab," I catch myself saying. Mary puts her hand on my knee and thanks me. I'm confused about why I offered to pay and even more confused about what to do in this situation where Mary's hand is on my knee. I opt for a smile and drink of my beer. Her hand stays on my knee the entire time while I sit frozen upright in my chair. This would be a good time to have something meaningful to say, but all I can think of is small talk. All I can think about is pointless questions about how she likes the new photocopier at work or what her plans for the weekend are. So of course, I manage to say nothing.

"Glad you made it out tonight. We all thought you were starting to turn into Dave." Mary finally takes her hand off my knee, just in time for the waitress to return with our drinks. I push my beer aside and go directly for the rum and Coke.

"Turn into Dave?"

"Yah, into a workaholic. You know … working away all the time, never going out. You seem to be spending a lot more time in your cubicle or at home. You used to be around a lot more."

"Has anyone ever invited Dave out? Maybe he doesn't have anything better to do."

Mary laughs and uses both hands to hold her straw while she takes a sip. "He's too much of a dork to go out with us."

Suddenly I pity Dave. He has done such a good job of pretending to be happy about not fitting in that people are able to rationalize excluding him.

"Wait, so is he so dorky you don't want to hang out with him, or is he dorky because he doesn't want to hang out with you?"

"What?" Mary sort of laughs, but her annoyance rings through loud and clear.

"Well, I mean is it a catch-22 situation here? We think Dave is a loser, so we don't invite him out, and so he doesn't go out, and so we think he is a loser. So is it our fault, or his?"

"Both, I guess." I've done it now. Mary is pulling away and growing disinterested. Nothing like killing someone's buzz with critical thought.

"Let's not talk about work. I see Steve and Jeff are faring pretty well over there."

Mary glances over at Steve and Jeff. "I wonder what they are talking about." Mary isn't alone in wondering. I look over and see the girls laughing with

Steve and Jeff; what could they possibly be saying that is so interesting? And why is it that every time I open my mouth, cynicism pours out and knocks people away?

"I imagine they're not discussing literature." I try to lighten the mood and hope that if I keep drinking, maybe I can at least try and sustain idle, more … fun … conversation. Mary smiles and pushes farther back in her chair. She is starting to scrunch her face and spread her attention around the room. Mary is formulating an exit strategy. Here it comes. Grasping the cuffs of her sleeves laying limply across her lap, she pulls the sleeves tighter around her waist. Then Mary stands up.

"I've got to use the washroom. I'll be right back." Mary doesn't let go of her sleeves until she's well clear of me. Her sweater hangs down from her hips and obscures any view of her posterior. An effective defensive strategy.

How people spend the entire night talking about so little is a mystery to me. When I listen to the conversations surrounding me, all I hear is people taking turns reciting monologues. One person starts talking about himself. Pause. The next person starts talking about herself.

"I had such a shitty day yesterday," says a woman to her friend.

Her friend can hardly wait to get a word in. "Oh *me* too! Let *me* tell you what happened to *me*."

What I hear is a woman reaching out to her friend for a compassionate ear, but she is quickly met by disregard and self-interest. All around the pub I can hear the same battle for attention in each conversation. The thought of someone telling me a frivolous story about some stupid misunderstanding or drunken escapade makes me shudder.

If only I were a little bit taller, maybe my life would have turned out differently.

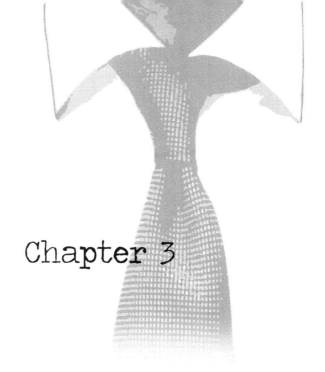

Chapter 3

I don't dream much anymore. Every night I close my eyes only to be greeted by the back of my eyelids. Recently, I've started wondering if that's all I am doing … staring at the back of my eyelids all night. I can feel the cold, tough exterior of my sheets against my skin while I lay in bed. Despite my best effort to stay still, I hear the noise my skin makes as it rubs up against my bed sheets. How can my body possibly make noise when I am lying motionless in the sheets? It's impossible to remember when I fall asleep at night, and it is often quite startling when I wake up to my alarm. It's as if after a few minutes of staring at the back of my eyelids I am suddenly transported into the future at the exact moment my alarm clock turns on. This morning I am woken up by an unwelcome conversation between two excessively chipper people talking about the most meaningless events of the past week.

A celebrity couple just broke up, despite being perfect for each other.

Some dweeb's wife left him after he spent their joint savings turning their home into a replica of the set of Star Trek.

Barack Obama chose to use an un-American brand of mustard for his hotdog.

I can only imagine that somewhere a woman is sitting at home alone with her radio on. She has just fed her cat and she is now writing an email to her friend. In the email she details how it's every guy's fault that she is alone and miserable. The radio provides the soundtrack to her typing as she sidesteps reality, fully convinced by the false narrative she has woven in the email to her friend. She nods her head approvingly of every criticism spouted by the radio people and is satisfied that somewhere out there, someone else is more pathetic than her. At least she never transformed her living room into the bridge of the starship Enterprise.

I find myself emotionless and robotic in the mornings.

Shut off alarm.

Swing legs over side of bed.

Sit up.

Not happy.

Not sad.

No thoughts.

Begin preparations for day of responsibility and obligation.

Once I'm out of bed and moving, taxing thoughts begin to surface. I am so tired of constantly having to do something, of always needing to be in a place where I have no influence or control. I don't pick the time. I have no say in what day. It especially doesn't matter what I want to do; someone else has already decided how fifty hours of my week will be spent.

I have the ability to shape my morning before work, and yet I drone through the same routine to keep my chorus of thoughts silent. I eat a bowl of cereal, shower, and put on my work clothes. In the mirror I watch myself fight the battle against gingivitis, lethargically going through the motions. Every scrape of the bristles against my teeth echoes throughout my modest, but clean, bathroom. The pace at which I move the brush back and forth slows as I become more aware that I am just watching myself; eventually, I am not even moving my arm anymore. I am standing and staring at myself in the mirror. All my mornings are the same. This is a reality that I have grown accustomed to, and only a small part of me laments my complacency.

Comfort killed curiosity. Rest assured, the cat is safe.

I am very careful to leave at least a fifteen-minute gap between when I eat and when I brush my teeth. I don't want all the chewed up bits of cereal still fresh in my mouth to get all over my toothbrush. I like to eat my cereal at the dining table without reading or watching anything. There's something about the sound of chewing in the quiet of the morning that I enjoy. It is something I might even say that I look forward to. The shower is probably the second most disappointing part about the weekday morning for me. The most disappointing part of my weekday morning is having to get out of bed on someone else's terms. The second is not the shower itself, but knowing that I have to eventually leave the warmth and comfort of the shower to put on a dress shirt without wrinkles. Wrinkle-free doesn't exist and ironing only seems to work until you put the shirt on. So, I either pick the shirt that annoys me the least or else I avoid looking in a mirror.

The daily commute to work is a quiet and prolonged period of escalating anxiety where it sinks in that my entire day is fucked. I pull out of my apartment parking lot and merge into morning traffic, gripping my steering wheel tight, my muscles stiff from the tension building about the impending small talk that awaits me at work. I'll hear every last detail of Mary's dinner. She'll reminisce about that incredibly funny thing her dog did.

"Oh, he's such a character," she'll exclaim.

Oh, *please tell me more.*

It's only on the way to work that I hope for every intersection light to turn red. I feel my fingers go limp around the steering wheel as I approach the fourth intersection on my morning trek. I look up at the intersection light and start to slow my speed by easing my foot off the gas pedal. I'm now in the intersection and directly underneath the shimmer of another green light. My grip around the wheel tightens, turning my knuckles white.

Four opportunities to delay the inevitable denied.

Unfortunately, time always seems to go by faster on the way to work. I want the morning drive to feel like forever. I'd be satisfied spending the rest of my time behind the steering wheel listening to classic rock and feeling the breeze blow in from my open window. But before I even have a chance to breathe during my morning commute, I find myself sitting idle in the parking lot at work. I turn the key in the ignition and shut off my only chance of escape. It usually takes about five minutes to digest and accept the disappointment that every decision I have ever made has led me to this point – this single, insignificant act of parking my car just to work aimlessly at increasing the profit of some organization that would replace me in a heartbeat.

The pursuit of income has supplanted the pursuit of happiness.

Without looking I navigate my hand along the inside of the car and find the handle to open the door. Pulling the handle, I feel the rush of fresh air breaking into my car. I take a deep breath and spring myself up out of my car to start my day. In the distance I see a few coworkers with coffees in hand, waddling back and forth with their heads slouched forward and their feet dragging across the pavement as they slowly make their way to the main entrance. It's oddly reminiscent of a documentary I watched on penguins.

Closing the car door and soaking in my surroundings, I'm struck by the sheer scope of effort humanity has put forth to physically get to work. Thousands of cars litter a giant concrete pad and I can only imagine that this pattern of waste repeats across the globe. Entire plots of land, home to thousands of organisms, are paved over so we can allow our pollution propelled contraptions to sit idle all day. It's odd that advertisements portray a car as a symbol of freedom and individuality. We're sold the idea that a car lets us go anywhere, anytime, and in any of the four available models. No one seems put off by the inherent irony that the freedom of mobility comes at the cost of dependence on gas and financing. You can go anywhere, anytime, as long as you can pay for it. Suddenly, your paycheck is that much more important and your car is relegated to your daily work commute. The car is a deal struck with the devil. An idea of freedom that will forever be just out of reach.

The preeminent truth of our time is that no one can escape the economy. Feudalism didn't dissolve with the industrial revolution; it simply evolved to fit the modern world. We are still indentured servants, tied to our debts, obligated to our lords at work, and strung along by the promise that one day we will be released from servitude if we work hard enough, long enough.

Will I ever earn my freedom?

A man named Gene Rosellini tried to find freedom from the spread of the modern world. He abandoned the trinkets of society and spent two years in the wilderness trying to ascertain whether or not humans could ever go back to living independent of technology, modern conveniences, and society. His final assessment: no. He committed suicide shortly after, maybe as a reaction to his depressing discovery that man has become dependent on *trinkets*.

I do my best to be discrete in the morning. I park in the furthest section of the furthest lot to the side of the building. Others will spend any amount of time driving up and down the front aisles of the parking lot to avoid a long walk from their car to the front door. I always make a point to avoid entering through the front door with everyone else. Instead, I walk the longest route around the back of the building and enter through a small door that leads to an emergency stairwell. My aversion to people in the morning feels like it qualifies as an emergency so I feel justified in my use of the emergency stairwell. My careful routine allows me to enter work unnoticed every morning, mostly because no one is looking for me, but also because no one knows the back door exists.

These fat bastards never take the stairs.

I get the sense that everyone is brought down each weekday morning by the death of their childhood dreams. No one spent their childhood dreaming about working a nine-to-five desk job. It just sort of happened. It's one of those unfortunate happenstances the universe doles out without remorse. Some people get to be rock stars, and the rest of us get to sit behind a desk and fantasize about being rock stars.

I can hear dissatisfaction in every footstep and every quiet sigh released as people sit down in their chairs for the first time each morning. I hear each chair wheeze under the load of its occupant and I hear the same sentiment expressed by the sitter of the chair, but then I hear silence. Sometimes it feels like a full minute between when people sit down for the first time and when they actually start doing something at their desk. Television has a lot to do with this awkward moment of silence. Television gives us an unrealistic portrayal of how life *ought to be,* and this tends to be far from the truth. Television never shows anyone working hard through the day or fighting lower back pain caused by extended periods of sitting. Television does nothing to prepare us for the many years of our lives spent paying bills and debt at the expense of our personal lives, and television does nothing to prepare us for the experience of not always getting what we want. Probably the worst thing television has done is influence our dreams. We dream about being rich, popular, and heroic instead of dreaming about trying to make the best out of our unremarkable lives. Television makes us feel like we've failed if we don't manage to have a happy family, great job, and constant adventure. Television doesn't encourage us to dream about making the world a better place for the people around us; television encourages us to dream about making the world a better place for ourselves. Everyone on TV somehow lives in great houses and apartments. These living spaces far beyond the reach of each character's purported occupation leave us insecure and dissatisfied with where we can afford to live. So in that one minute of silence between sitting down and getting to work, I imagine my coworkers are thinking about everything they aren't. They are thinking about all the adventures they've seen on TV but will never get to experience. It's pretty easy to identify what we aren't, but much harder to come to terms with what we are.

Everything you become is also everything you will never become. The opportunity cost of living.

9:00 am. I find myself looking at my wrist watch every few seconds, but my eyes never seem to be able to focus. The numbers are a blur, but I keep looking anyway.

"Great night on Friday, eh?"

I don't know how long Jeff's been standing over my shoulder, but he seems quite comfortable leaning against the outer edge of my cubicle entrance.

"Yah, not too bad. Though I can't seem to remember much." Normally I lie to get through small talk, but as the words come out, I realize I really can't remember what happened Friday night. I know I went out, I know I met Jeff at O'Flaherty's, but after talking awkwardly with Mary, all I can remember next is waking up.

"I don't doubt it. You were all kinds of drunk." Jeff's stupid subtle grin has now blossomed into a full grimace. "After a few drinks you really relaxed. Then after a few more drinks you were actually fun. You should maybe consider drinking more often. Alcoholism might actually be a good move for you."

"I didn't do anything stupid, did I?"

Jeff pauses, he seems to be thinking. I'm mostly concerned about whether or not I told anyone off.

"I think you might have hit on Mary a little bit too hard, but I think she thought it was pretty funny. Despite you flirting like Forrest Gump, you two hung out pretty much all night."

"Mary?" I can feel my stomach sink. This must be what it feels like when you swallow your pride. Not that Mary is unattractive, but I can imagine this will make things pretty awkward between us at work. Not to mention I still can't picture what her butt looks like.

"Maybe I should apologize." I shrug my shoulders and make my best attempt at looking honest.

"Dude, don't even worry about it." As Jeff brushes aside my concern, Steve worms his way past Jeff into my cubicle. In the little space I have, there are now three guys pretending to be comfortable with the closing distance between genitals.

"There he is. Give this guy seven or eight beers and he's actually alright." Steve gestures towards me. "Thanks for sitting with Mary all night. Normally we need to make sure we keep her company, but having you there really freed us up."

"Yah it did. How about those two girls. Foxes." It's as if I'm no longer in the cubicle with Jeff and Steve. They are talking directly over me.

Steve smiles and pulls out his phone. "Look at this text I got from Michelle last night." Steve holds the phone so only Jeff can see it.

Jeff giggles naughtily, if that's even possible. "Was that her name? I thought it was Richelle."

"How many girls have you met named Richelle?" I interject. Both Steve and Jeff laugh. I ask, "You guys never make a move on Mary?"

"No way." Jeff is quick to answer. "First rule of working in an office: never sleep with your coworkers."

Steve cuts in, "It never ends well."

"Well," Jeff hums slightly as he thinks, "I suppose if you're willing to make a commitment it could end OK."

"Like I said, it never ends well," Steve repeats.

Jeff laughs. "Plus, Mary is just a bit too plain." Steve picks up right where Jeff left off, like they share the same mind but talk out of two different mouths. "We like flashy girls. You know, blonde, put effort into what they're going to wear. It shows they care."

"It shows they care about what?" I sound bitter.

Steve grunts. "There's nothing wrong about wanting to look good. I appreciate a girl who looks good, and I'm sure they appreciate when I look good."

"I wonder," I lean forward in my chair, careful not to lean into Jeff's or Steve's dick. The lean fails and makes everyone feel slightly uncomfortable, so I retreat into a casual backwards tilt and quietly mumble, "Does it even matter what you talk about when you meet these women, or is it just a matter of getting through the formalities until it's appropriate to go home with each other?"

"If you have to ask, you'll never know. But hey, I gotta take off. Got some reports to push out." Jeff pushes off the edge of my cubicle and casually walks away. I don't know how he managed to make that exit look so cool, but I've never been more envious of someone walking away before. It's just Steve and I in the cubicle now. We share a brief moment of eye contact before Steve leaves me with his parting remarks.

"Mary seems like the right girl for you. She dresses boring and you are boring. You could have boring kids and stay in on weekends. Grow duller together. Sounds like a dream."

9:15 am. I find a fixed point on my desk and stare at it. It's a small, yellow note, and it's right in the middle of my desk. To the left of this note is my computer, to the right a stack of neatly organized papers and my stapler. The note sits alone on the cold laminate desktop. Strange that I didn't notice the note until now, but it's all I can focus on at the moment. I pick it up off the desk and bring it close enough for my eyes to focus. There seems to be a message written very small in black marker.

"I'm going to kill you last."

9:16 am. Every muscle in my body tightens and every breath becomes a painful chore as my eyes study every curve and line of the small black lettering. I keep waiting for a laugh, or someone to pop out from around the corner to point out how gullible I am.

Nothing.

I'm overwhelmed by the sound of silence. I can't make out a single noise in the office. No more voices, no more toes tapping, no more keys being struck – just my thoughts and the sound the note is making as I hold it in my hand. I focus on this apparent threat on my life, or joke in poor taste, and try to elicit an emotional response. I want to feel angry and crush this note in my hand, yet I am unable to move. The more I concentrate on the note, the louder the silence becomes, and the more my muscles tighten. I am a statue, struck in a stoic pose that hides the calamity beneath.

Why do I often feel like I am watching a scene in a play or movie unfold instead of living and acting in real-time? I'm in the audience, unable to interact with the characters. I can only watch my life play out and ruminate on what I feel should have happened. Right now I want to see a show of confidence. I want this note crumpled up and thrown on the floor in a show of power and grace. Instead, what I see is a slow motion shot of the note being placed in a field of paper and pens spread across my desk.

9:20 am. I can't be the only one who wishes they were someone else.

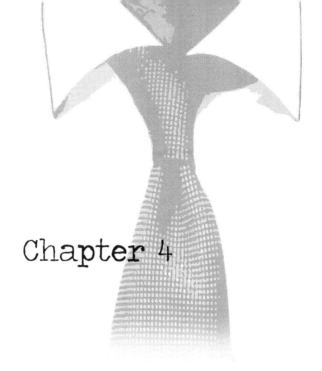

Chapter 4

I'm tucked away in the corner of the lunchroom eating a sandwich by myself. I snuck in about five minutes after everyone else and sank down into an empty seat near the pop machines. The pop machines vibrate so loud that you need to shout to have a conversation, making cola corner the least desirable piece of lunchtime real estate in the room. When someone buys a pop, the thud of the can dropping from the innards of the machine is enough to overpower any voice. It's not a quick thud you can pause momentarily to accommodate. Instead, there's a long and drawn-out series of clicks and clacks, then a sharp mechanical whine just before the can is released for its elaborate descent during which the can seems to hit an impossible amount of edges before reaching the bottom. It's not uncommon for the cans to explode after opening, so purchasing is a risky decision. It also makes for a great game of chance, playing the percentages on which cans will burst.

I'm very good at going unnoticed at lunch, or maybe no one cares to make conversation with me. Either way I get my wish and eat in silence. I put on a pair of earphones, stare at a faded, chipped white wall, and imagine myself staring at a chipped, white wall in the Kennedy Space Center cafeteria. It's a realistic fantasy, since I'm already in a cafeteria, but I feel more important staring at a wall associated with launching spacecraft. Advancing the frontier of science by pushing beyond our terrestrial border feels more noble than advancing the value of our companies stock on the open market.

My life may be on the wrong trajectory.

I remember when I first started working here. I'd sit in the lunch room without any earphones, listening in on everyone's conversations. Not like a pervert holding a cup against a wall, but more like an airline passenger with no choice. The lunchroom sounded like a group of adults talking to babies with everyone raising the pitch of their voice, slowly enunciating every word, and becoming unreasonably excited about every detail shared.

Phonies.

Fakes.

It's been a few years since I started working here. The lunchroom remains a daycare for invisible children. Adults grit their teeth and nod aggressively as they wait their turn to talk. Pain pours out from my colleagues eyes as they force their cheek muscles to smile. There's no denying people are insincere. It's funny to watch people work so hard to care about what others say. It is unrealistic for anyone to be so excited listening to stories about someone else's weekend.

"I took my kids to the zoo this weekend," I hear one person say.

"Ohhh, w-o-w that is *sooo* wonderful! I bet they *reaaaally* liked it." This person could be talking to a four-year-old and I wouldn't be able to tell the difference.

"I took my kids to the movie theatre, bought them some popcorn."

"Mmmmmmmm, yum! That sounds like a *greaaaat* time. I bet they *really* just enjoyed that *sooo* much." *Like,* gag me with a spoon …

It's disgusting listening to the way everyone pretends to care about each other. I prefer the overwhelming hum of the pop machine to the adult baby talk that dominates the staff lunchroom and hallways. So in go my earphones.

When I shut off the sound and observed my coworkers lunching, patterns started to emerge. Routines for where people sit, who they sit with, who does all the talking, how they place their food on the table, and when they go for coffee repeated daily. I'm watching the same lunch play out over and over again, blurring the line between today and yesterday. At the centre of the lunchroom is Jeff. Not the physical centre, but Jeff has an aura that pulls people in. He is personable, funny, good-looking, and everyone wants to be his friend. The fact that Jeff goes out of his way to invite me out or to talk to me in my cubicle is something I can't understand. Fortunately, Jeff leaves me alone during lunch to keep his social capital from plummeting on the open market.

Never present in the lunchroom is Dave. Like myself, the Slave prefers to eat alone, only he chooses to do it from the privacy of his cubicle. Dave seems like the kind of guy that is happy about being a workaholic, believing that if he works hard enough he will one day get the promotion he deserves. Unfortunately for Dave, he is meek. Management can sense meekness the way a shark picks up the scent of blood in water. The meek shall inherit dead-end jobs. The workplace is a gladiator arena where employees are pitted against each other in a battle of accomplishment to win the favour of upper management. He who wins over upper management is sure to earn a ticket out of the arena and into a private office on the top floor. To win in the arena you have to do more than produce good work – you must endear yourself to upper management by over-exaggerating your daily contributions and efforts. Dave is neither warrior nor showman and he will never win the favour of upper management.

Maybe Dave wrote the note. He's quiet, repressed, overworked, and meets all the Google-search criteria for a disgruntled employee secretly plotting to shoot up his co-workers. He probably got beat up in high school for doing well on tests. His reward for doing homework, studying, and getting good grades was being pushed around and taunted by kids who didn't have the drive to work hard in school. I've shirked him on numerous occasions in the office. The rudeness I've shown the Slave has likely reserved me a special spot on his killing list. Or maybe he knows how much I hate everyone, and he is generous enough to afford me the kindness of seeing everyone else die first before he gives me what I deserve.

The other day I saw Dave walking towards the office entrance juggling a briefcase, several large binders, and a coffee. Steve was holding the entrance door open for some girls walking just ahead of Dave, but as soon as the girls made it through the door Steve just let it shut in Dave's face. I watched Dave wrestle with the binders and coffee as he struggled to open the door. I also watched the person standing behind Dave wait quietly. As soon as Dave managed to open the door, the person pushed right past him, splashing coffee on the Slave.

Small slights cut the deepest.

About ten minutes through lunch the office kitchen becomes completely empty. The only reason to use the office kitchen is to sidestep work by wasting as much time as you can brewing coffee, but at lunch time the kitchen is completely abandoned for the comfort of the staff lunchroom. I just can't stand the thought of the poor kitchen being all alone at lunch, so I like to visit and carry out minor acts of office terrorism to keep the kitchen in good spirits.

My favourite target is the staff coffee machine. It's where the drones collect to renew their collective spirit of compliance. Without coffee, a drone becomes wrought with exhaustion and feelings of dissatisfaction. The hive mind requires we consume ourselves fully with work: the more we prove ourselves to be good worker bees, the more the hive requires of us. A good drone is encumbered with obligation, task-driven, and too tired for personal pursuits. To gather energy for work, most consume coffee. The common trope, *I'm useless without my coffee*, is part of the collective consciousness. Drinking coffee blocks the uptake of chemical signals that alert your brain of exhaustion, thereby building up the reserve the more you drink. The damn breaks when there is not enough caffeine to fortify the walls – releasing a flood of headaches, drowsiness, and lethargy. We boost our energy to flourish at work and once we finish we are left fighting the broken dam.

The gift of rejuvenation only costs your dependence.

I believe in dealing with problems passively aggressively, so I protest coffee culture by mixing soil into the ground coffee. Walking into the kitchen, I set my lunchbox down on the countertop beside the coffee machine. I unclick the metal locks on the outside of the handle and flip the lid over to reveal the apple and plastic container of soil that lay inside. Reaching up into the cupboard above the coffee machine, I grab the large container of coffee. This container is freshened up weekly, usually with some generic brand purchased with our office supplies, but occasionally someone will bring in their personal blend, something expensive and eclectic. A common complaint in the office is how bad the coffee tastes. I've seen new grinds brought in, machines replaced, and filtered water introduced to the brewing process, with only temporary results. No one can figure out why our office coffee tastes so bad. Most people are so desperate they drink it anyway, adding more sugar to improve the taste. Opening the lid to the coffee I pour in a bit of the soil, close the lid, shake, and repeat until I am out of soil.

Most days I choose to perform simpler acts of unkindness. A daily favourite is randomly moving items in the fridge around. I'll swap the contents of lunch pails, remove labels, switch the contents of the salt and sugar dispensers, take beverages out and leave them on the counter, and do anything else that may cause someone to distrust a coworker. Today I've decided to grab everyone's afternoon banana and squeeze lightly, applying just enough pressure to cause the banana to turn mushy without causing unsightly brown spots on the outside. Bruised and mushy bananas make me gag, so I assume it must do the same to others.

12:50 pm. I head back to my desk early to avoid having to talk to anyone in the hallways. I think that if I sink low enough in my chair, maybe no one will notice me. It's been days since I've done any real work and no one seems to care. I open a document on my computer and stare at my cursor icon as I swirl it around in endless circles. Some days I'm not even sure what my job is. Today I've opened a database for a recent acquisition we have been assigned to support. The company I work for assists companies in acquisitions and mergers, and what I'm looking at is the complete financial history of some drilling company based in Alaska. I'm expected to sift through hundreds of lines of financial data and present a strategy for gutting its operations. Success in today's economy is for thin companies. These are companies with small payrolls, limited concern for safety, disregard for the environment, and an aptitude for dodging taxes. We live in a sociopathic world. We create and support large corporate efforts to destroy and undermine society, we allow a select few to profit and grow rich from abusing the majority, and we tear down anyone who complains. The world won't come to an end because of a comet or the wrath of the four horseman of the apocalypse; no, the world is going to end because of our inability to be objective.

I'm finding it harder than usual to relax at my desk. For one thing, I can't seem to find the ominous note anywhere. I pick up my trash can and sift through it, nothing. I open every drawer in my desk, move around every object, and look underneath whatever papers I come across. Nothing. How can I not remember where I put it? Whoever wrote it must have taken it back. Fucking Dave – he's the only other person in the office who doesn't meander in the break room during lunch. He always arrives at work before me, he could have slipped it on my desk this morning while I was still sitting in my car and then taken it away while I was squeezing bananas.

"Hey!" Steve slams his hands on my desk, shooting me a playful grin. "What the hell you doing, you look like you're working on a philosophy degree here."

"What?" This is the best response I can muster after being taken by surprise.

Steve rolls his eyes and lets out a sigh before explaining himself. "You looked like you were hard at it, you know. Deep in thought. Bad joke, I guess. Anyway, grab your shit. You better be done with your efficiency recommendations for that specialized parts company because our meeting's this afternoon."

In reality, only a fraction of a second passes, but its passing is as slow and uncomfortable as a discussion about sex with your parents. "That's today?"

"Yah, it's today. You better have your shit together. Dave and Jason present right after us. Idiots, like they got a shot at providing better recommendations than ours."

Dave. His name echoes through my head. "What do you mean, Dave and Jason?"

"Boss wants to lean out and cut the fat kids from gym class. So those of us who provide terrible recommendations aren't helping the company streamline and make a profit. If you don't put beef on the table, then get the fuck out of the butcher shop. I wouldn't be worried, though. Jason's a pothead and Dave is practically invisible."

"Don't worry … I have my work ready." I smile in a vain effort to look confident. Steve would be able to see right through me if he wasn't so busy trying to be casual about eyeing up every girl in the office.

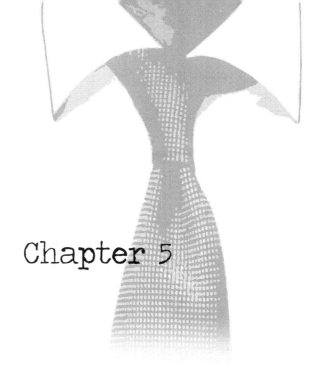

Chapter 5

1:15 pm. One hour until Steve and I present to our dickhead boss. But instead of reviewing notes for the presentation, I'm slouched in my chair trying to be discrete about the glue I'm applying between pages of the office printer paper. Running my fingers across the ridges of the hundreds of sheets of paper, I stop randomly, peel back a few layers, and rub circles with a glue stick onto the page. I do this a few times until I feel like I've stuck enough pages together to cause a few paper jams. If I'm lucky, I'll be around to watch someone in the office struggle to remove the paper jam caused by the stuck-together sheets as they pass through the guts of the printer. It will most likely ruin someone's day and maybe even cause a sharp enough decline in office productivity to irritate our boss, Reid.

"Dave, isn't that the fourth time in a row you've worn that tie?"

"Yah, don't you have any other ties? Or is this the one that brings you all your luck?"

I overhear two guys talking down to Dave. I can't see them, but it's obvious from their guttural laughter that they think what they're saying is hilarious.

The Slave responds cheerfully, "I just really like this one." In tone Dave may sound like he is in good spirits, but I can sense the angst behind what he is saying. Some men have no fight in them; they are indifferent to the forces that keep them down and they just hope to make it through the day without being hurt. The sad irony is that by avoiding pain, these people open themselves up to pain. These are likely the same people who don't vote and accept unfair policies in the workplace because they don't see how it will make a difference. *What difference will it make if I complain? What will fighting back achieve? I'm better off keeping my head down.*

Apathy has never been a solution to any problem.

Everyone in the office can hear these two men harassing Dave, but no one cares enough to do anything about it. Like Dave, everyone wants to avoid putting themselves in a situation where they may have to face pain. But you can't be a hero without accepting pain. You can't grow without pain.

"Diversity, Dave. That's the key to success." I can hear more laughter and a noticeable wheeze coming from a congested nostril. "You really ought to freshin' up your look. Take Phil, here: how many shirt, tie, and pant combos do you have, Phil?"

"Well fuck, Greg, I've got too many to count. Thirty ties, fifteen pairs of pants, twenty shirts, that's got to be a few hundred possible combinations of great looking attire. Some of those pants are one hundred percent wool. They breathe and goddamn if I don't look good in them."

Someone must be rubbing their tie with their fingers because I can hear the gruff scratch of skin against fabric in the background. I picture Phil flaunting his tie between his fingers, petting it like that James Bond villain stroked his cat. Real sinister.

"See, Phil here is ready for any occasion. Valentine's Day, boom! He puts on a pink dress shirt with a red tie. Important investors are in town?" Greg humps the side of Dave's cubicle and moans, "Ohh! Crisp white dress shirt with pinstripe, bold tie and fitted, light grey jacket and pant combo, 100% wool. That's why he's on top and you're where you are. Because he looks fucking good."

"I like to think my work ethic weighs a little more than looks." Dave wants that statement to be true, but experience should have indicated otherwise to him. Uniforms impress people. Whether you are a pilot, soldier, firefighter or Wall Street banker, if you look the part, people will treat you like the part. If you look like an average person, you will be treated like an average person.

"Work ethic. Right." The laughter coming from the two men slowly fades as they walk away. If karma was real, something terrible would happen to those two men, but karma is not real. Karma is an excuse. I have no love for Dave and I'm almost convinced the Slave penned a death threat to me earlier today. But I do feel pity for him. I also have an innate hatred of guys who are better-looking and more successful than me, especially when those guys flaunt their good looks and money unapologetically.

I slip the stack of printer paper back in its original package, use the glue to reseal the flaps, and pencil a small line across the side of the label to mark my work. After scrawling a line I pause, looking around to see if anyone is watching, I quickly slash a few pencil marks to turn the line into a Z. It feels as cool as I thought it would. Only a keen eye would notice that the package of paper has already been opened, and only a super sleuth would spy the Z blazed in pencil. Fortunately, no one really cares to pay attention to little details like the packaging printer paper comes in. Sliding the pack of freshly ruined paper to the corner of my desk, I play through a few violent scenes in my head. Greg and Phil have cornered me at the water cooler. They're wearing their typical designer clothes, Phil is jerking off his tie between his fingers, and they are looking to boost their manhood by stepping on me.

"Look, all I want is some water. Why don't you two go tell some stories about how awesome you were in high school at a gym shower somewhere." I put my paper cup under the tap of the cooler and poor myself some water.

Greg sticks his arm out and leans against the wall behind the cooler. Leaning over me, he grunts out, "Are you calling us fags?" Phil puts his hand on the water cooler, leaving me sandwiched between two assholes.

"Actually, I'm calling you guys assholes." I stand up confidently between Greg and Phil. "But you sound pretty defensive about your sexuality." Raising an eyebrow, I raise my arms in front of me and thrust my index fingers suggestively into each other.

Phil snaps, "That's not even how gay sex happens."

"Oh, my mistake. I must not have as much experience as you." I try to walk away but Greg pushes me back into the water cooler. Though it's only a daydream, I can feel myself tense up with rage. I push my forearm against Greg's collarbone and shove him hard into the wall. Phil panics as he watches Greg squirm when I press into him with my forearm. I lean in close to utter some clever threat but I can't think of anything to say. The intense satisfaction

I am feeling about pushing Greg into the wall is ruined. What would Arnold Schwarzenegger say? *"Cool off."* Then throw a cup of water into Greg's face.

My daydream has fizzled out because of my lack of creativity during the crowning point of the confrontation. I hate guys like Greg and Phil. I'm jealous of guys like Greg and Phil. I envy their good looks and I hate how they constantly get away with treating everyone around them like shit. I know karma doesn't exist because Greg and Phil bully, taunt, lie, cheat, and steal, and yet they always seem to be rewarded with good fortune. I want the worst for them and I am not going to apathetically wait for fate to take action. Fate has no power if people aren't willing to make decisions, because fate is really just after the fact validation of outcome. No more daydreaming, no more watching – I am going to do something.

I have become retribution, the destroyer of ego.

As much as I'd like to inflict pain on Greg and Phil, they are stronger and would most likely kick my ass if it came down to physical blows. I need to fight clever like Muhammad Ali. Ali didn't just train hard in the gym and hope his technical ability would let him defeat one of the most physically intimidating boxers of all time. To beat George Foreman, Ali knew he had to negate the attributes that made George Foreman a devastating fighter and not simply hope he'd be fast enough to dance around his forceful blows. Ali trained with heavy hitters and spent hours a day getting pummelled in the ring to get used to the feeling of being beat on by a bigger man. When they finally fought in Africa, the force of Foreman's punch didn't intimidate or push Ali around. For likely the first time in Foreman's career, he experienced an unsettling panic because his greatest attribute wasn't going to get him his way. Ali targeted Foreman's confidence and slowly tore him down by demeaning his proudest attribute.

If Greg and Phil use their good looks to get their way, then I'm going to have to show them what it's like to not be able to rely on physical appearance to stand on top of others. I want them to feel as insecure and vulnerable as the people they taunt and push around. I want to let them know how it feels to be undesirable.

Cat piss. What an idea. I'll never forget how awful it smelled when some kid's cat peed on his coat in the eighth grade. It was like the kid was surrounded by an invisible force field that just pushed people away from him. No one wanted to sit near him or talk to him, but everyone wanted to talk about him. The stench grabbed the attention of the class and caused everyone to spend their day shooting him disgusted looks and whispering nasty things. All it took to replace the history of friendship between this kid and his classmates with contempt was a mighty pungent scent. All the good looks in the world couldn't buy this kid a friend that day; even the teacher asked him to go home because of the disruption he was causing in the classroom.

I'm not quite sure where I'm going to get cat piss, but I'm confident that some pervert on Craigslist will sell it to me. I open up the outdated web browser work allows us to use and start the process of loading. According to management, there is almost no reason for any employee at work to use the internet other than for email, so we are provided computers that are too old to use the plug-ins necessary to load most content from web browsers. I'm also positive that the impossibly slow internet connection we have access to is the result of our office using lite internet. Lite internet shouldn't even exist as an option for consumers. High speed internet is not a finite commodity; in fact, all it takes is a phone call to have some call centre jockey activate your high speed internet. A technician doesn't even have to enter your home or fiddle with your modem. All it takes is a phone call to change your account information and suddenly it's like the magic wizard blocking high speed internet from passing through your ethernet cable is knocked off the path.

You shall not browse!

After four agonizing minutes I am finally able to post an ad on Craigslist.

Wanted: Fresh jar of cat piss. No questions.

Offering: $25

Contact: …

Exhaling, I ponder the contact information field. I don't want to deal with regular messages to my email inquiring if I need a top up on cat piss and I don't want anyone adding the cat piss guy to Facebook through my email. I should do what most people do when they want to get into some weird shit on the internet and create a fake email account. What would be a good email address, I wonder? It should probably come across as friendly and reassuring. *Catluver33.* The use of a "u" instead of an "o" makes the fake address seem creative and friendly. People can trust someone creative enough to purposely misspell words on the internet.

Catluver33 needs to buy some fresh kitty urine.

After thirty minutes I finally get my post up on the internet. How long does it take for someone to respond to an ad like this? Is there someone actually waiting to sell their cat's piss, or will my ad simply spark the curiosity of some woman low on money but high in feline friends? Time will tell. Maybe I will even fall madly in love with the woman who sells me her cat's urine.

The internet is the unconscious mind of society. All the dirty thoughts we try to suppress find articulation through anonymous postings on open forums and perverted websites.

Chapter 6

F ate favours those who are born into affluence. Even ugly, talentless, and insufferable people benefit greatly from fortune. If I could point to any instance to disprove the existence of God, it would be the continual success of rich kids who lie and cheat their way through life. Money has a way of buying success and friends that hard work and generosity seldom achieve. Hardly seems fair, but there's little point in getting bent out of shape every time the world is unfair.

I am sitting in an excessively large boardroom. A long, smooth rectangular desk separates Steve and I from our boss, Mr. Philip Reid. Reid is one of those ugly, talentless, and insufferable rich kids that blossomed into an entitled assbag. Garbed in designer suits and charioted through the city in an imported luxury car, Reid looks like an important man. Centuries ago, kings were bred into their roles not because they were the most competent, but because they happened to be ejected from the right womb. Reid is a lasting remnant of ancient times. He is a leader thrust into his role because his parents had been successful in life, not because he earned or deserved it. All Reid had to do was show up and go through the motions. His cockiness doesn't even allow for the thought that he might not deserve to be where he is today to percolate in his dense mind.

"You have thirty minutes," Reid announces with little expression in his voice. His face is stiff, his arms are crossed, and his eyes express how demeaning interaction with his employees is to his hubris.

Like trained lapdogs we stand and give our presentation. Countless hours at work are spent seeking the approval and affection of our employers. We might as well be house pets because we are just as domesticated: broken in by teachers, adopted by employers, and allowed to play in the park with the other company pets. Money is the leash that keeps us from running away. Money keeps us from venturing to somewhere we'd likely prefer to be, and money is why we continually drain our spirits plugging away in affordable, polyester shirts. I think it wouldn't bother me so much if I wasn't the only one who noticed. No one else seems to mind that someone else is holding our leash because they think that work provides meaning in life, that work defines who we are as people. The perceived meaningfulness of a career provides clarity of purpose and direction. Work is a distraction from life. We're being tugged on by our leash to avoid straying away from the path that was built for us. We never learn what's beyond the path, and we never learn how to be useful to ourselves. There is no meaning to be found in my work. My job does not define me, nor does it have any bearing on who I am as a person. My job restrains me and exhausts my will. I'm too tired to make anything of myself after work hours and I'm too beaten down emotionally and mentally by the time the weekend comes to find peace of mind. How am I ever going to find any meaning in life if I never have an opportunity to live my life? I am alive outside regular working hours, yet I exist in relation to the workday.

"Interesting," Reid's comment refocuses my attention to the presentation.

Steve and I were required to develop a creative strategy to save a failing company that we've been tasked with selling. Clemmon's Systems Components is a national company that had humble beginnings. It started as a family business, building custom components for gas and fluid systems. After winning major contracts within Detroit they sprung up factories all over the United States. But the economic downturn has not been kind to Clemmon's, and this has resulted in several years of unprofitability. Instead of facing adversity, the owners decided to sell the company and let someone else figure out how to thrive in a dwindling market. That is where Steve and I come in: we review every last detail about the operation of the company and find a way to make the company successful – or at least create a convincing enough argument to motivate a buyer to purchase the company. Clemmon's will likely be swallowed up by some international organization intent on furthering its monopoly in a niche market. The economic downturn was actually a blessing for businesses like ours. Struggling entrepreneurs contract us out to alleviate them of their burden, and big businesses wait eagerly for us to present them with our fresh stock of failing companies.

"How do you plan on motivating the workforce? If you eliminate jobs and reduce benefits, while increasing demands, you will likely find staff unmotivated to perform at the level you require."

Steve freezes. From the expression on his face I gather that he did not expect Reid to ask that question and so he is struggling to articulate a response.

"The Hawthorne effect." I break the nervous silence with the first thought that crosses my mind, a surprisingly clear memory from the intro to psychology course I had taken in my undergrad. Reid and Steve focus their attention on me.

"...The Hawthorne effect? Care to elaborate?" Reid's left eyebrow raises in a way I've never seen before. This must be what it looks like when he is interested.

"Of course." I take a deep breath and prepare to test my memory and back up my hasty comment. "In psychology there is a term that describes skewed results in research regarding performance. What researchers discovered is that people work harder and perform better when they are given special attention. So let's say you agree to have a third party come in and do a study on factory productivity. A third party conducting a study would require researchers to enter the factory and observe the performance of workers. Well, studies have shown that while being observed and rated employees will work harder than they normally would. If the results of the observation are positive, they stand to benefit or at least feel an increased level of pride. It can be any kind of special attention; it doesn't have to be a research study. You could move the supervisor from a secluded office to the main floor. Hire someone to constantly watch the employees. Increased supervision doesn't sound like a great idea, but that is because you are likely imagining the traditional watchdog supervisor. If we install a supervisor that encourages and recognizes good work with verbal prompts, or even written compliments, then we might be able to encourage employees to perform. You could even be generous and provide nominal recognition like small, one-time pay bonuses to staff rated highly by the supervisor. Employees will compete against each other, achieve a sense of pride in their work, and receive intrinsic satisfaction from knowing they are doing a good job. This may only provide short-term increase in productivity before employees begin to burn out, but it will probably be long enough a time span for us to sell off the company." Steve looks as if a chimpanzee just scored a checkmate against him, a mixture of disbelief and awe.

"Interesting." Reid scribbles some notes on the pad of paper in front of him. He is the most animated I've seen him since our presentation started. "I think I've seen what I need to for today. I've got a copy of your report and presentation with me. Expect follow-up from me within the next few days."

We talk about people as if they are just a variable that needs to be manipulated to attain desired results. We have a complete disregard for the welfare of people and an infatuation with profit.

When did output become more important than people?

Chapter 7

Returning to my desk I find a reply from Craigslist waiting for me in my inbox. Apparently MizzWhiskers113 has what I need and is willing to sell it to me, tonight.

I will sell you cat piss. 100 bucks if you want it tonight. Message me back and I will tell you where you can meet me.

A hundred dollars seems rather steep for what I'm looking for, but it's not like there's a thriving market of packaged cat piss I can use as a price point for negotiation. I could hold firm on twenty-five dollars, knowing that anyone willing to get their cat to pee in a container for a stranger must be desperate, but MizzWhiskers113 has earned this hundred dollars from me with her firm approach.

$100 is fine by me. Where do I meet you?

Whoever is on the other end of this conversation must have been waiting eagerly for me to reply because in the time it takes me to palm my face and rub the soft spots under my eyes I've received a reply. MizzWhiskers is instructing me to meet her in Vickers Park at the bench on the north side of the duck pond. I guess I can't say I'm surprised about the location an internet stranger provided me to meet her at, but I will be surprised if she's brushed her hair.

I've got a lot of time to kill until seven tonight and my uncreative mind can't think of a way to keep myself busy. By the time I get out of work and make it to Vickers Park it will likely only be quarter to six ... I could get some food and wait it out in my car, but some overzealous mother might spot me sitting alone in my car and think I'm a pedophile. It's just one of those unfair things about life when you're a guy in your late twenties: if you spend time alone in public, everyone will assume you're some lonely creep. But if Forrest Gump can sit alone on a bench in the park, then I see no reason why I can't sit and wait an hour or two at the park. Instead of a box of chocolates, maybe I will just pick up some Thai in one of those fancy boxes. There's nothing creepy about a man trying to eat rice out of a box with two sticks on a public bench.

Several hours pass and now I'm sitting beside an empty takeout box in Vickers Park. Ducks are waddling around me, hoping I'll toss them some food, but I've got nothing for them. I don't even know what the hell ducks eat. They are always waddling but I never see them eat anything but bread from old people. I reach down to the ground and tear out some grass to throw at the ducks. As I sit back up, I notice that someone has taken the empty seat on the bench beside me. I inspect the girl who is now sitting on my right to see if she meets my expectations. She is wearing large sunglasses, her hair is pulled back in a well-kept ponytail, and she is dressed in light blue jeans with a baggy brown sweater. Seems normal enough.

"So are you from the internet?" I figure being direct will get me the answer I want. This isn't a date, so there's no need for tact on this occasion.

"I'm actually from planet Earth, but I've spent some time on the internet." She tips her sunglasses forward and makes eye contact with me. "You the creep who's willing to pay a hundred for cat piss?"

"I guess it won't mean much to you if I say I have a completely reasonable reason to be buying cat piss."

"No. Not really." She reaches into her purse and pulls out a container wrapped in a plastic bag. "I don't really care what you're using it for."

I see her smile as I pull money out of my coat pocket. "Well, it might be creepy to buy cat piss, but you're the one selling it. I guess that makes us both creepy."

She lets out a sigh as she sticks the money in her purse. "Yah, well sometimes you gotta get creative to make some money."

MizzWhiskers isn't entirely unattractive and she makes a good point about needing to be creative to make money. I can't help but wonder what would have happened had we met under different circumstances. Maybe we could have been friends.

"You sell cat piss much?"

"First time," she grins, "I'm hoping this turns into a lucrative business for me. It's something my cat does on the regular."

"Any chance you'd like to grab a drink?" Considering she's the first interesting person I've met in recent memory, I figure I might as well try asking her out. I'm barely able to finish my thought before she starts laughing.

"No." MizzWhiskers tilts her head back and continues to laugh. It's safe to say I feel like an idiot and can't wait for her to walk away and let me be.

"OK." I can't believe she's still sitting on the bench … *Go away, go away, go away*, repeats in my head while I grind my teeth and stare at the pond. After a minute I look over to see what she could possibly be doing still seated on the bench. After all, *I was here first.* She's pulled out a bag of shredded bread and shows no signs of leaving. She's just tossing out bread to the delight of all the ducks.

Without looking over at me she slurs out a lethargic prompt. "So, are you going to leave or do you enjoy being awkward?" A few ducks waddle towards her feet.

"Funny, I was just wondering the same thing. Well, thanks for the piss. Hope your husband Mr. Whiskers doesn't mind you selling it to me." I get a handful of bread thrown into my face and an angry stare for that comment.

The eight-year-old in me wants to throw a pile of grass in her face and run away; unfortunately, the adult in me decides to thank her for the jar of urine and walk away quietly. My eight-year-old self just called me a pussy.

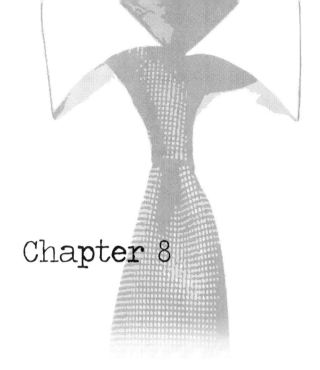

Chapter 8

I find myself sitting in the dark, relieved to be alone, at home. I'm reclined in my brown leather reading chair mindlessly playing with a small object in my hand the same way someone with restless leg syndrome twitches their foot for comfort. The object is light, thin, and the sharp edges flick nicely against my fingers. I reach out with my free hand and pull the cord of the lamp beside me. *And God said, let there be light.* As I tug the cord my apartment quickly becomes illuminated by the faint glow of the reading lamp. My apartment is tidy and organized. Every piece of furniture and object is carefully placed and orderly. Some might describe my apartment as basic or lacklustre, but I like to think of it as functional and modern. Every item serves a purpose and no frivolous decorations clutter my personal space. I don't purchase art, nor do I pad my shelves with books I've never read. What my apartment says about me is that I am most likely a boring person.

I look down at what I had been playing with and quickly recognize it as the yellow note from this morning. I scan my memory trying to find the moment when I slipped this note into my pocket. Frustrated at my inability to remember anything, I crumple the note and throw it as far away as I can. I must be full of cat-piss confidence because I actually managed to squash and toss the note. In the dim lighting, I see the oblong outline of the note sitting on my floor in stark contrast to the tidy arrangement of furniture. It wasn't quite the dramatic display of confident defiance I had previously pined after. I had expected that I would be overcome by a cathartic wave of relief after tossing the note, but I find myself doused with disappointment. The note should beg questions: Who wrote it? Is it real? Should I be worried? Instead, I am more concerned about how confidently I can dismiss the note and move on.

As much as I'd like to be nonchalant enough to allow the note to sit on my floor until it simply breaks down into nothing, I can't. My apartment may give people the impression that I am boring, but at least it also gives the impression that I am capable of cleaning up after myself. Forcing myself from the chair I make my way to the note and pluck it from the ground like a weed.

I'm going to kill you first.

Staring at the note, my mind immediately spells out the name D A V E. I've finally moved off critical examination of my reaction towards the note into the questioning the identity of the author. Dave the Slave, disliked at work, and most likely candidate to lose his job despite being the hardest worker in the office … he must have written the note. He knew I was giving a presentation today that would likely result in him losing his job. Maybe he hoped the note would throw me off, or maybe he gave notes to everyone in our office.

"I'm going to kill you first."

"I'm going to kill you fourth."

Maybe he numbered everyone in the office. Dave is the type of person to consider every detail and put in the extra effort necessary to not only number each victim, but to provide a courteous warning of their impending end.

My train of thought is abruptly cut off by a vibrating sensation in my pants. It doesn't take long to identify the source as my cell phone, but it takes a few seconds longer for me to remember what to do when someone calls. Answering the phone, I manage to grunt out an unimpressed salutation,

"Hullo."

"Hi, I'm calling on behalf of Morley Bank, we have an exciting offer for life insurance that…"

Without hesitation I cut off the caller: "I'm not interested."

"You haven't heard our limited time offer, just for you."

I let out a snort, "I don't need to. If I die, I prefer to leave nothing behind for anyone to take. If I die I want to burden everyone else with the responsibility of repaying my loans. I want my next of kin to regret my financial decisions as much as I do." There's a silent pause. The operator can hear the words I'm saying, but it's clear she is still determined to make the sale. After all, she won't receive a treat from her owners unless she manages to sell me life insurance.

"Well how…"

Before the operator has a chance to finish her sentence, I hang up the phone and end our brief relationship forever.

Life insurance. Perfect way to keep the masses petrified about money. In death everything that we are ceases to exist, except our debts. Our debts are passed on for our closest relatives to worry about. We're told that if we truly care about our loved ones, we'll pay a small fee every month for the rest of our lives in anticipation of the inevitable. We spend our lives pining after what society tells us we need: houses, cars, nice clothes, and travel plans to tropical beaches. We become indebted to the rich in order to pay for our conditioned wants, and in the end we are left with no option but to plug away in a time-consuming job so we can afford our lines of credit. Not even in death will the rich forgive our debts. The last thing the world expects is some outlandish loner willing to rack up debt without leaving anyone behind to pay for his mistakes. The only "fuck you" to the world I can think of.

I need to get out more.

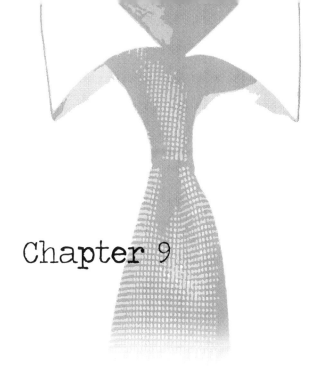

Chapter 9

8:30 am. I am starting my work day in the office conference room surrounded by coworkers and boxes of donuts. Watching my colleagues eat donuts is like watching a weird rollercoaster of sensual emotions. When they pick up the round pastry, time seems to slow down. I watch as they close their eyes and breathe in all the rich aroma of the donut. Slowly the donut edges closer and closer to their lips, stopping just before penetrating the inside of their mouth. If you listen closely you can hear them whisper quietly, *just one bite, one bite won't hurt*. There's a brief pause. Then just as the donut nears the lips, the eyes explode open and the mouth lusts after the sensation of sinking into the soft skin of the donut. The first bite is far from modest and sends a pleasurable shudder through the eater's body. *Just one more bite and then I'll stop* … but there is no stopping. The last bite of the donut is followed by a satisfied groan that quickly turns into a disgusted whimper. *I shouldn't have eaten that whole donut.* A few minutes pass and you can almost hear the negotiation happening internally. *Well, you've already eaten one donut. One more can't hurt. You've come this far.* With a strained face and a reluctant, jerky motion of the arm, another donut is plucked and consumed.

In addition to donuts, staff meetings are generally a forum for unwelcome news and the introduction of new and unpopular policies. Waiting for us when we enter the room is a neatly stacked pile of papers on the large conference room table. The woman sitting behind the papers decides to pass the time by distributing them to everyone in the room, which she is much too enthusiastic about doing. Alive with cheer, this woman ceremoniously licks her finger each time she passes a page from the pile of papers in her hands to someone seated around the table. The corner of each page she distributes becomes dense and heavy with saliva. After each person in the room has received a sheet of paper, she realizes that there is more than one page that requires circulation. She pauses momentarily to rebuild her store of saliva, and once again begins licking her finger and rubbing spit on every page she dishes out. It's socially unacceptable to lick your palm before shaking someone's hand, but apparently I should not be concerned that someone has just lapped the corner of a page I am required to touch. All I can do is hold the paper pinched between my thumb and index finger with my arm extended away from my body. I scrunch my face into a sour frown. The paper is in the foreground, but my line of sight is focused on the lady gleefully spreading her spit all over everyone's papers. Either the castoff taste of the paper on her finger is causing her mild tones of joy, or she gains a sadistic glee knowing that in a roundabout way she has just spit on all her coworkers. I notice a few colleagues eyeing me. The manner I have chosen to hold the page in front of me must look peculiar to them, so I gently place the page on the conference table without ever taking my eyes off Margaret.

"Is everything OK?" Linda puts her hand on the table in front of me in order to gather my attention.

"Everything is great," I smile at Linda and reach into my work bag that I placed on the floor beside me. I'm not clear what I'm reaching for but I figure it will provide a suitable escape route from conversation with Linda. Digging deep in the bag I can feel the silhouette of a pen. I pull it out of the bag and rest my arm on the table with the pen clutched firmly in my grasp. I look over at Linda and smile as I start clicking the pen with my thumb. It makes a loud springing sound as I flick the edge of the push button. We've been told in numerous meetings how distracting and inappropriate it is to click our pens during conversation; this signifies disrespect and can easily overpower any discussion. The incessant clicking sound subverts the intended focus of the dialogue and brings your conversational partner into a fit of quiet rage.

"That's … good." Linda is smiling, but somehow her teeth are showing. She looks like someone slipped something painful into her gums and the only way to remove it is with her lips. She is now solely focused on my thumb as it clicks the pen. Conversation avoided.

A hush falls over the room as Reid steps through the doorway upright and uptight in his expensive designer suit. Reid walks towards his seat at the head of the conference table and swings his leather briefcase over the table's edge. With great care and precision Reid slows the momentum of his arm and allows the briefcase to touch down softly. Reid looks like he wants to say something but is too distracted. I catch him glaring at me and my pen as he descends into his giant rectangle of a chair. It resembles the black monolith in 2001: A Space Odyssey, except with protruding armrests and a landing pad for your butt. I am seated in the shadow of his monolith at the other end of the conference table and now everyone in the room has joined Reid in staring at me. It's as if the room has tilted in my general direction. This is my moment: like Rosa Parks I could remain in my seat, refuse to conform, and continue clicking my pen resolutely in the face of adversity. When Reid directs me to *"Stop causing a disturbance, and please focus on the task at hand"*, I could respond by standing up in defiance, or remain seated. Rosa's defiant stand was actually a long period of sitting, since she only stood up metaphorically. So, like Rosa, I can take a metaphorical stand and lean back in my well-padded simulated-leather chair, hold my arm up high, and click my pen with determination and defiance. Every click embodies my protest.

Click, no I will not be told what to do. A sequence of slow, drawn out squeaks follow the near unison pivot of people and pleather chairs towards Reid.

Click, click, my respect for you is fake and the result of coercion. A collage of heads and backs paints my field of view as my colleagues choose to face away from me. Turning away from what makes you uncomfortable is an easy route to relief, though you never really resolve the malaise stemming from your passivity.

Click, everyone in this room belittles you behind your back. Click. Click. I can only imagine the pleasant veneer facing Reid now, mostly because everyone is facing away from me and there are no mirrors for me to confirm what I believe to be transpiring on the faces of my colleagues. Playing nice to stay on his good side they are likely smiling and hoping I'll stop acting out. This could be our moment. If everyone would just grab their pens, we could take control of this meeting. We could show Reid we won't be bullied any longer.

Click, click, click, the only reason we behave is because we fear we won't be able to find anything better. No one will stand with me. No one will say no to coercion.

The plight of white collar workers, putting in forty plus hours per week for minimal pay, dismal benefits, and diminished personal lives, is not considered a social issue. I am not Rosa Parks, and I am not allowed to be dismayed by my prospects for the future, so instead of taking a stand I put my pen down and retract my arm in defeat. The atmosphere in the room levels off to an even keel, and this allows Reid to return to his position of power. There is no point in questioning the routine work week or stagnant wages. Never mind that there has never been a study indicating that forty or more hours a week is optimal in terms of employee productivity, or that forty plus hours a week for minimal pay is beneficial for the economy.

Don't challenge the status quo.

Employees were blessed with the five-day work week in a grand concili-ation by Henry Ford and his conciliation was widely adopted by Western society as the gold standard. While parts of the Western world slowly reduces the amount of hours it requires people to commit – all while increasing annual income – North America is discreetly increasing the required hours of employees through salaried positions and avoiding any significant increase in compensation. Employers might claim that they cannot afford to hire more people and pay better salaries, but that is contradicted by the fact that the average CEO in America now earns more in one day than the average worker earns in an entire year. The gap between rich and poor is steadily increasing and no one cares. Following the 1950s North America experienced several decades of increased quality of life for the average person due to fair income distribution and taxes placed on the wealthy. This resulted in a reasonable wage gap between the rich, middle class, and poor. The rich in America have managed to subtly reclaim their historic place of privilege and this time they mean to keep it. To the rich, the middle class are fraudulent aristocrats stealing their rightful wealth.

"The company has not been performing on par with projected quotas." Skipping the formality of introductions, Reid immediately delves into business.

"As a result we have been looking for redundancies and unnecessary expenditures so that we can make up for the loss in revenue." Reid moves his briefcase slightly to the left, but makes no attempt to open it.

"We will no longer be covering the cost of food, alcohol, or supplies for staff gatherings on select holidays. Instead you will be asked to bring in your own supplies at your own cost. Additionally, we have had experts provide us with manageable quotas for office supplies you are permitted to use within a year." Reid finally opens his briefcase, providing an opportunity for the staff to exchange dismayed glances.

Pulling out a stack of papers, Reid motions for the person to his left to begin passing them out. "On this sheet you will see a breakdown of supplies you are permitted to use per day, per week, per month, and per year. Staples, pens, paper, ink, and electricity are not free. Your irresponsible use of these items has cost the company money, and our lack of performance has necessitated that we bring your abuses under control."

I don't imagine Reid's annual bonus was ever on the table for reduction. It's much more reasonable to only allow me to use three staples per day than to not pay out a five hundred thousand dollar bonus to Reid for telling us to do work that we already know we have to do.

"Please ensure you review the memo before the end of the week. There is an addendum to the memo that was circulated before I entered the room. The addendum is a formal acknowledgment that you've read and understood the conditions listed in the memo. I recommend you have it signed and submitted by Friday. If you have any questions, you can contact Human Resources." Reid closes his briefcase and ends his interaction with us. Looking up from his briefcase I catch Reid scan the room, his eyes darting between the mangled remains of donut scattered across the conference table. A slight wince appears in the upper left part of Reid's mouth before he pulls his briefcase off the table and power walks out of the conference room.

Steve turns towards me, "Well, at least they aren't asking us to ration the toilet paper."

"I'm sure it's on here somewhere." Jeff peers closely at the ration list.

Steve lets out a sigh. "Well, they say employees do better when they have defined tasks and boundaries. We should probably be superstars with these kinds of boundaries."

Everyone around the table is now fully engrossed in deprecating jabs about our place of employment and the restrictions listed in the ration list. Everyone around me is either releasing repressed anxiety about work, categorically listing off everything that work has done to piss them off, or trying to find a new way to say the same thing as someone else in a slightly different tone. In a strange twist of fate, I am sitting in a slightly reclined position with my arms crossed and an emphatic smile stretching from ear to ear. No one at the conference table notices me watching them, nor do they seem to hear the slight chortling noise emanating from my grin. If someone starts crying I may not be able to contain my laughter. Strange that I should find so much pleasure in this scene playing out in front of me. There's a sort of joy knowing that everyone feels the same way I do and that I'm not the only person who is unhappy.

"So at what point do we go back to work?" The cathartic release of pent up emotions is brought to an abrupt end by Mary's question, and my amusement withdraws with the ensuing silence.

"We should just stay here for a while. Impromptu staff meeting." I can't place the name of the girl who just spoke up. I've never learned her name because I've always made a special effort to avoid her. She smiles too much. It can't be possible for someone to be *that* happy all the time, so my conclusion is she must be some sort of psychopath. At some point in her life she must have been convinced that you need to smile in public or people won't think you like them. This notion has become so engrained in her subconscious that she wears a constant smile out of fear that she will send the wrong message to the people around her. With such a neurotic compulsion to smile in the company of others, I bet she even feels the need to smile in the presence of her cat. It would be a tragedy if Mr. Mittens felt like she didn't love him because she wasn't smiling at him.

"Well," Jeff gathers the attention of the room, "we probably could have gotten away with that, if we had all stayed here."

"Aren't we all here?" I'm not sure how this girl manages to talk through her smile.

"Not quite. It seems the Slave managed to sneak away. He's probably telling Reid about how all of us are bitching about him. What a rat." The group has shifted their hatred of work towards their hatred of Dave.

When the mob feels threatened, dissenters like Dave are promptly lynched.

Chapter 10

G reg and Phil brush past my cubicle on their way to the elevator. I assume they are heading downstairs to the overpriced coffee shop across the street from the office, which leaves me about fifteen minutes to discretely rub cat piss on their chairs. How one goes about looking wholesome while holding a container full of cat piss is beyond me, but new experiences are the fruit of life. Sweet and healthy. I'm not just using a paintbrush to baste Greg's and Phil's chairs with cat piss out of spite, I'm basting their chairs because I believe in living a healthy life, replete with rich, new experiences.

I'm crouched forward in my chair, half tucked under my desk, grasping a lunch pail with the brush and container in it. A man holding a lunch pail in an office setting isn't anything worth taking note of so I should have no issue transporting my wrath to Greg's and Phil's cubicles. Taking a deep breath I visualize my path to Greg's cubicle. Ten steps forward, turn right at the weird fake tree, then walk straight until I reach the window. Greg is the first (or last, depending on your perspective) cubicle on Scenic Row. Scenic Row is where all the jackasses with large windows overlooking the misplaced display of nature on the office front lawn sit. The building I work in is surrounded by concrete, strip malls, and tall buildings; the only green spaces visible in the area are the ditches that hug the road on either side and the odd forest situated at the front of our building. Rows of trees, green grass, and wildflowers stand in stark contrast to the urban sprawl that surrounds the area. From Greg's point of view, work is a bright, colourful place that sways with every breeze. Too bad the cubicle walls on Scenic Row act as a barrier that blocks any potential cheer from spilling out to the rest of us.

"You stupid bastard." I can't avoid mumbling these words as I drift into Greg's cubicle. The colours. The beauty. My hands are shaking, but I don't know if it's anger or awe that is coursing through my hands. The safe bet would be awe-inspired anger. Standing on my tip toes, I peer over the top of Greg's cubicle on the lookout for any witnesses. Nobody. Hunkering down, I peer at my watch and laugh.

"Of course." It's break time. Everyone is allowed to leave their desk for fifteen minutes without an excuse during break time. There isn't a soul in sight.

"Meow," I sing as I open the container of piss and swirl the brush around, making sure I saturate the bristles thoroughly.

"Mr. Whiskers thinks you've been a real son of a bitch, Greg." With a grin that stretches from ear to ear I start basting Greg's chair on all the pressure points where his body hits. The arm rests, the two indents where his buttocks rest, and the lower lumbar support comprise just enough surface area to get the smell on his clothes without causing too much panic about any dampness. As I step back from his chair I notice his jacket on a coat hanger near the cubicle entrance.

"When in Rome." I dip the piss-soaked brush into the pockets of his coat and stroke it up and down the inner lining of the sleeves carefully while making sure I don't get any on myself. Fortunately for me, Phil occupies the cubicle beside Greg's so I don't have far to travel to repeat the process. It only takes a few minutes to leave a moist trap for Greg and Phil, but the satisfaction from this new experience will leave me tingling with satisfaction for hours. I just hope they aren't deterred from sitting down at their desk by the new pungent smell that cropped up during their short break.

There's a noticeable pep in my step as I make my way back to my cubicle. My arms are swinging and I'm borderline ready to start whistling some Styx: "Too Much Time on My Hands" seems to be the unavoidable soundtrack playing through my brain. When I reach the cubicle intersection with the weird plants, I'm forced to twist my body sideways to avoid colliding with Greg and Phil. They barrel past me without any concern for my existence.

"Cocksuckers," I mutter with my shoulders pressed against a cubicle wall as I'm forced to yet again move out of someone's way while walking. It's always me, always, always, *always* me that has to move out of the way. It's like I'm invisible.

Chapter 11

I often close my eyes at work and hope that I'll disappear. I am constantly disappointed when I open my eyes and find that I'm still sitting at my desk being suffocated by the tight collar of my dress shirt. I can't seem to shake the feeling that I am floating my way through life. Like a passive viewer, I am just watching life unfold rather than living as an active participant taking control and making decisions. I struggle to feel a connection to anything or anyone and I feel no desire to be any different. Sometimes I wonder why it always seems to be so strenuous to connect with the world around me. To care about work. Maybe my stubborn nature precludes me from the accepted social practices of others.

"Jesus, man, you look terrible."

I must look as bad as I feel.

Steve lets out a sigh. He grabs a stapler from my desk and starts fiddling with it. "You been having trouble sleeping or something?"

"Well, Steve. To be honest, sleep is really the only thing I enjoy doing. If anything, I've been having trouble not sleeping. Shit keeps happening that prevents me from being able to sleep in or nap during the day. My body doesn't quite understand why I continually deprive it of sleep. I'd try to explain to my body that I have a day job, but I just don't think it'd understand."

Putting the stapler down, Steve forces a cautious smile. I don't think he can tell if I'm making a joke or trying to express personal feelings to him. Expressing personal feelings to a male co-worker would be a major breach of workplace man-to-man interaction etiquette. To ease the growing tension, I perform the traditional dance of friendly banter. I begin fiddling with a pen and laugh playfully. It's important to fiddle, otherwise it looks like you don't care about resolving awkward tension.

Steve quickly relaxes and joins me in laughing. "Yah, who doesn't enjoy sleeping. Christ, I'd be sleeping right now if I could."

"Yah," I try my best to smile and make eye contact. "Well, I really gotta get back to work here."

"Yah, same here, thought I'd just drop by." Steve returns my smile. As he starts to walk away he stops and suddenly jolts backwards. "Hey man, you want to grab some drinks with some of us after work? Maybe you can hang out with Mary again."

I'm not sure how long I hesitate before answering. To me, it feels like at least three minutes. Although, had the pause gone on that long, I'm sure I would have noticed an unpleasant reaction in the facial expressions of Steve.

"Sure. I can't think of a reason why not." That's a total lie. I have plenty of reasons why not.

"Cool. I'll give you a shout later today."

"Great." After obtaining a satisfactory answer, Steve finally leaves. I wonder, do I hate socializing, or do I just hate that I'm not good at it? Now that Steve has gone, there is nothing to distract me from the tasks I should be completing. I am behind on my work, and I seem to be getting even more behind every week. If you created a graph to visually display my productivity throughout my time as an employee here, let the x-axis represent every day I've been at work since I've been hired, and let the y-axis represent each hour I spend at work, you would notice that the line representing my productivity is on a downward slope. With each passing day I manage to stretch the boundaries of wasting time and ignoring responsibility.

Procrastination. It's like a disease. The onset of procrastination is so protracted that it often goes unnoticed as it grows and methodically infects your personality. The signs are subtle. A missed bill payment on Tuesday.

Lying in bed an extra ten minutes and arriving to work late on Thursday. If left untreated, procrastination will leave the body incapable of acting out on will, and the mind will just turn into an empty chamber. Too lazy to think or care, just the reverberating echo of the brain trying to activate the chemical processes necessary to spring the body into action. I am in a depressed state of inactivity caused by demands that have slowly become unmanageable. Everyone thinks procrastination is just a phase and that eventually they will get their act together and break the cycle, but that's a lie. A disease like procrastination feeds off denial like mould consumes an aging piece of fruit. It doesn't stop. It progresses until it consumes the fruit wholly.

By the time the symptoms become pronounced enough to notice your crippling neurological disease, it is likely too late. My mind and body become exasperated by the smallest action. Going to work becomes so taxing that all I can think about is going home, lying on the couch, and doing nothing. Every minute that passes my body becomes heavier and my thoughts become more lethargic. Seeing past today becomes so strenuous that the future no longer has any bearing on my life. I am static and too tired to imagine a future. When you stop dreaming because you can't seem to find the resolve necessary to activate your limbic and paralimbic systems, then you've reached an impasse. If a doctor were to examine you, they would likely say that you are alive. Your heart is pumping blood to all your vital organs, your lungs fill and empty with air, and you are capable of responding to queries. For all intents and purposes, you are functionally living. But you no longer have any dreams or aspirations. All you look forward to is shrinking away from the world. You wake up on a Saturday morning and can't even find the motivation to feed yourself breakfast until you are starving, and even then you struggle to find the energy to make something worth eating.

I have a disease that no one can see, and I suffer in silence.

Chapter 12

10:50 am. It's going to be a long day. I can feel it. The impending sense of longevity in the air makes my clothes damp and heavy. Every second demands my attention just so it can flaunt how slowly it is passing. I'm left with two options in this predicament: either I can enjoy the fact that time has slowed down, thereby conceivably bringing me closer to immortality, or I can deal with the unresolved issue that is causing my perception of time to slow down.

Dave and his goddamn note. With the conviction of a religious zealot I pound my fist on my desk. I am ready to commit myself to an action based on a bold assumption that I don't have verifiable proof to back up. But to hell with it: I believe that Dave penned that death threat and I am going to confront him about it, regardless of evidence.

Wheeling my ergonomically-designed bonded leatherette chair away from my desk I erupt into a steadfast upright position. Standing provides me with a vantage point of the office which sitting, by its very nature, had withheld. Peering over my cubicle wall I see busy little worker bees making honey for their queen. I see Jeff trying to charm a client on the phone, Mary making a concerted effort to look interested in what she is typing, and Greg and Phil walking around the aisles casually sniffing the air. I wonder if they smell something ... I feel my heart rate rise. Every thump gets louder and faster and I frantically start looking around the office. I see so many unfamiliar faces. Who are these people, and what are they doing? Why are they here? Why have they never mattered to me before?

I start the slow walk out of my cubicle towards Dave's desk. Gathering steam, I am on an unavoidable course for confrontation. On an average day, I'd do my best to avoid any human contact that wasn't absolutely necessary for the completion of my day, but today is a good day to switch it up. I'm only a few steps away from his desk now. Each step I take on the carpet screams with determination. If Dave has any ability to sense his surroundings, he must know I am headed in his direction with a purpose.

"Hey Dave, I know it was you." My body is half-draped inside his small cubicle. My right leg is positioned across the entrance and I'm doing my best to appear intimidating.

Dave turns his chair. He seems genuinely surprised to see me.

"What do you mean?"

"The note. I know you left the note to fuck with me. Well, your plan's backfired. I know what you're up to."

"Honestly, I have no idea what you're talking about. What note? What is it you think I'm up to?" I start tapping my fingers, creating a small cascading sound effect on the side of Dave's cubicle. My impatience couldn't be any clearer.

"The yellow post-it note, Dave. You put it on my desk the other day. I know it was you. You're either trying to screw with me, or you really are crazy and you're planning to kill everyone in the office."

"I'm sorry, what? Kill everyone in the office? I ... don't even know how to respond, are you on drugs?" A long pause finds its way between the staredown Dave and I are locked in. I'm fairly impressed with the fact Dave hasn't looked away. I always figured him to lack the self-confidence necessary to really look someone in the eye. My body is overcome with rage. I feel my fingers shake and beads of sweat slowly trickle down my back. I want to tear down the walls of Dave's cubicle and grab his little head and press it against the cold hard surface of his desk. I want to push his head into his desk so hard that the stupid arrogant look on his face turns into an anguished plea for mercy.

I close my eyes and try to calm myself. Tapping the finger of my right hand on the upper edge of Dave's cubicle entrance, I open my eyes and force all my pent-up anger into words.

"You wrote that note." The elevated level of my voice echoes through the office. The busy little bees break from routine and freeze in panic after their daily routine is interrupted by my emotional outburst. Now everyone is confronted with the dilemma of whether they should intervene or pretend like they haven't noticed. I hear the electrons firing in their brains, sending the signal to pretend like nothing out of the ordinary is happening. Had Dave truly wanted to kill me, he probably could have shot or stabbed me right here and now and every single drone in this office would have attested that they saw and heard nothing. My death would be just as surprising to them as it would be to the dysfunctional family eating their dinner in front of the evening news.

I still can't detect any hint of recognition in Dave's eyes. He genuinely seems confused about my accusations. Lifting his hands up in the air he calmly tells me that he didn't write any note.

"Maybe if you have the note, you can show it to me. If I recognize the handwriting, maybe I can help."

I desperately want to stick the note right onto Dave's forehead. His calm, non-confrontational way of dealing with my accusations really irks me. I can't stand that he lacks the spine to stand up for himself. Dave should be telling me where I can stick the note and to get out of his personal space, but instead he is offering to help and attempting to make me feel understood. I reach into the pocket on the left side of my pants. Nothing. I reach into the pocket on the right side of my pants. Nothing again.

I let out a nervous chuckle as panic sets in. My hands are now frantically searching every pocket again and again, and frustration and confusion over-take my normally calm and expressionless face. For a few seconds the world around me is a blur of colour, texture, and sound. Like any adrenaline-induced outburst, this moment quickly fades and is replaced by the alarming sensation that everyone is watching me. Clenching my jaw and tightening my hands into fists, I manage to subdue my emotional outburst with uneasy physical tension. There's no recovering from this moment. I am now fully conscious of everyone in the room and can almost read how they are feeling. My only course of action is to simply walk away. No words or sleight of hand can help me save face in this incident. If any knowledge should be garnered from this interaction, it is that I am not as detached from emotion as I thought.

Dave's decision to wear a plaid tie with a boldly striped shirt is a major fashion faux pas. There it is, like a child who's suffered a verbal defeat, I've thought up my defence. I'd like to slam my foot down, cross my arms, and shout how stupid his tie and shirt look, then storm out with heavy steps. Instead I'll do the adult thing and walk away, scowling under my breath.

Chapter 13

Normally I hate sitting in the lunchroom, but today there's a show I don't want to miss. As much as everyone believes they've grown up and matured since high school, they haven't. Every office, workplace, and lunchroom cultivates the same bullying, gossip, and social stratification that high school is fabled for. Out of the corner of my eye I see Greg and Phil stroll into the lunchroom. Typically they wear a noticeable upward slant of their chin and a cocky strut bouncing from every step, but today they have their eyes on the floor and are avoiding any excessive swaying of their limbs and butts. Silence ripples like a wave through staff in the lunchroom as Greg and Phil walk past their tables. The smell of cat piss flowing off Greg and Phil is so off-putting that entire conversations are brought to a pause by the undeniable urge to gag. For the first time in their lives they are experiencing what it's like to be undesirable and to stand out for all the wrong reasons. To manage the anticipation of what will happen next, I start gnawing on my sandwich the same way a person in a theatre would stuff their face with handfuls of popcorn. I'm almost sent into a fit of laughter as they take seats at their usual lunch table and cause an immediate exodus of staff who had previously been sitting there. These aren't just random staff that decided to get up without providing the courtesy of an apology or eye contact with Greg and Phil, these are staff who sit with them every day. These are supposed friends and colleagues who spend five days a week together talking shit about other people in the office and making others feel miserable about themselves.

"I can't even breathe." The people at the table behind them are trying their best to breathe through their mouths, but it's a losing battle.

"It's just awful," I hear as each person at the table gets up and glares at Greg and Phil. They slowly shuffle and cough their way out of the lunchroom. I feel no remorse for the embarrassment I've caused Greg and Phil and I feel no shame for being a bad person.

"God, it smells like my aunt's house," blurts out one man as he gets up with the girl who was seated beside him.

Covering her mouth, she coughs, "It's like stale cat piss."

"Yah, exactly like my aunt's house."

Steve gets up from his table which is about three rows down from Greg and Phil, slides through the small crowd shuffling away from the hazard zone, and approaches the origin of the smell.

"Gee," Steve knocks his knuckles against Greg and Phil's table. "You guys really killed the lunch mood. New cologne? You might want to return it for something less risqué."

"You know what, Steve, don't wanna hear it right now."

"Yah well, I don't want to smell it right now. Maybe you guys should take the afternoon off, eh? Do us all a favour?" Both Greg and Phil put down their food and look up at Steve. It looks like they are having a difficult time acclimatizing to being on the receiving end of bullying. Meanwhile, Steve is doing an admirable job of deflating their egos.

"Relax, boys, I don't want any problems. You'd probably just wipe the smell on me anyway."

Greg and Phil both brace their hands on the table and slowly lift themselves up to face Steve eye to eye.

Phil barks, "You want to keep talking?"

"Why don't you boys stop pretending like you're going to do something and sit down before you get yourselves in trouble." Steve looks Phil straight in the eye and shows no sign of backing down. Phil takes a step back and sits back down with Greg following suit. Looks like Steve just won the showdown.

I lean forward in my seat and tighten the grip on my sandwich in suspense of Steve's one-liner that will bring the conflict to a close.

"Smell ya later." Steve walks away from the scene without even looking back, leaving two demoralized humans in the wake of his confidence. Steve notices me watching him walk away from Greg and Phil and gives me a quick wink midstride before suddenly bringing his body to a halt. He takes one step back and slides into an empty seat beside two attractive women. If anyone else tried to do what Steve just did, they would probably come across as a creep, but these two women smile and exchange excited glances. As I sit by myself in the corner of the lunchroom and watch Steve bring two women to life with clever comments and an overall ability to carry on a conversation, I come to the sad realization that Steve is the kind of person I fantasize about being. I don't hate him; I am jealous of him because he is everything people like. He seems to enjoy talking to people and people enjoy talking to him. Steve stands up for himself and women find him desirable. His hair is always so fucking cool, and despite wearing fitted dress shirts, he never has any sweat stains. I've never even seen a wrinkle on his shirts or pants.

What does it feel like to have everything go your way?

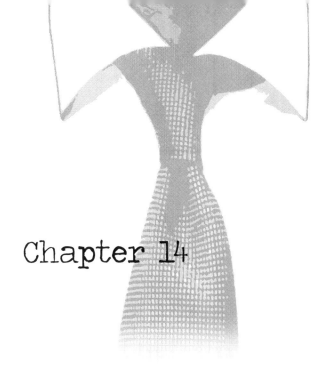

Chapter 14

I'm fixated on what the people around me are eating. I'm mesmerized by pub patrons pronouncing their freshly acquired dietary restrictions. Astounded by people manipulating their friends to cheat on their diets. It's a special occasion after all. Everyone always seems to be on a new diet motivated by some trendy celebrity fad. These trendy new diets are typically characterized by periods of extremes that can't possibly be sustained by any normal person.

Complete removal of carbohydrates from daily consumption, despite carbohydrates being a significant source of energy and essential for the development of muscle.

A diet comprised entirely of juices. No meats, dairy, or grains, just fruits and vegetables blended into puree.

No cooked foods, just raw food. This diet is especially effective if you happen to be a rabbit.

Consumption of twelve glasses of water mixed with maple syrup, lemon juice, cayenne pepper, and laxative, guaranteed to help cleanse your system. I think it's safe to assume that any sort of laxative will effectively cleanse your bowels of any unwanted substance. You can skip the rest of the gag-worthy ingredients and just dive right into the laxative, maybe cap it off with a gentle enema rinse.

Instead of maintaining a balanced diet and only eating junk food as an occasional treat, most people choose to eat poorly on a daily basis. Their over-the-top eating habits result in the expansion and softening of their bodies. Inflated like a balloon, they then turn to whatever new diet promises them the shortest period of separation from their junk food. Our ethos is rooted in reactions; we rarely look at life as an aggregate of choices.

"I'm fat. I need a diet that will get me into shape for the summer."

The problem with dieting to lose weight is that once you lose the weight you're likely to return to the same eating habits that led to the problem in the first place. Diets are not a permanent solution, and they do not address the problem.

"My daily eating habits are terrible and I don't even come close to participating in adequate amounts of physical activity. I make awful choices on a regular basis, and as a result I am significantly overweight, deprived of nutrition, and suffering from a lack of proper muscle development. I should make dramatic and lasting changes to the way that I live my life so that I can be a much healthier and happier individual."

I am looking at two large mammals hunkered down at their dining table at O'Flaherty's. The waiter drops off their order: each meal consists of a large burger and side of fries that consume the entire surface area of the porcelain plate. I can see the disgusting orange glow of the cheese as it dribbles down the edge of the burger and bun. I do very little to hide the contractions of repulsion I feel for these people from showing on my face. I can see Steve staring at me awkwardly; he eventually interrupts my targeted hatred with a well-timed joke.

"Well, at least they ordered the Diet Coke!" Steve slaps my shoulder, and doesn't seem concerned about whether or not I join him in laughing.

"Yah," I give Steve the glance I know he's looking for, and manage to force a convincingly friendly laugh. "It's a slow suicide. You know that on the list of the ten leading causes of death in America, eating habits are listed as number six? People poison their bodies with shit until their bodies just give up. The heart can't keep up when you push the boundaries of your personal circumference." *Reader's Digest*, full of useful nuggets of information.

Something about what I've said seems rather amusing to Steve, and he starts snorting and jeering. "I can picture the infomercial now. *Do you struggle not having heart attacks when you walk up the stairs? Do you find yourself crying uncontrollably when you get home and realize the fries you ordered aren't in your takeout bag? Thousands of Americans die every day, because they eat like shit. For just a penny a day, you can help them put the burger down.*"

From the corner of my eye I see Mary stroll in: she's wearing one of those excessively long and baggy shirts, yet again thwarting any bid to gawk at her glutes. "What's so funny?" Mary grabs Steve's arm to get his attention, her eyes light up with interest. "What did I miss?"

Steve looks over at me. "Oh, we're just being dicks." He shrugs. "Probably shouldn't be so mean."

Jeff goes on for a while about something, but I seem to have trouble focusing on anything he is saying. I'm bothered by his modest suggestion that maybe I shouldn't be so mean. Sounds simple enough: just refrain from blurting out crude comments. What comments remain to be made? It's hard enough to find things to talk about. Take away criticizing others, and what am I left with? Criticizing myself? This line of thought brings me to an alarming realization about my coarse thoughts. Is the fact that I have these thoughts mean that, at my core, I am not a good person? Are these negative thoughts reflexes emanating from the architecture of my brain, or have I directed effort into building up this muscle and training this into a reflex?

"Yeah, you can be such a dick sometimes." There's something about the way Mary casually looks up from her drink and flashes me a quick, soft smile before looking back at Jeff. It's not out of the realm of possibilities that Mary considers me a sexually viable candidate. What is it that makes a person want to have sex with another person? Is it strictly a result of biological happenstance? Pheromones in the air that happen to be palatable to your biological urge to procreate? Or maybe it's a case of vanity. People look for the most attractive sexual partners to build up their resume of sexual conquests. It's hard to believe personality ever really comes into play. Give a person a few drinks and they'll sleep with the most insufferable person if they are attractive. Let's be honest, a person who is unable to elicit even the slightest bit of arousal from a stranger with their physical appearance will not be able to motivate anyone to engage in sex with them, no matter how great a personality they have. Let's stop pretending we are anything but animals with a complex form of grunts, opposable thumbs, and khaki pants. Fortunately for the average-looking person, alcohol seems to lower the bar for physical expectations. The tainted sight of the inebriated stranger is nature's airbrush, making us all just a little bit more pretty.

I am sitting here trying to figure out why so many people spend so much of their time concerned about whether or not they will get laid and completely ignoring the advances of a relatively attractive woman. Steve and Jeff may find Mary to be too plain, but I find her attractive.

The overactive sexual urges of the human race must be the result of our primal desire to survive. We are like bacteria, breeding at every opportunity and slowly multiplying until we overtake the planet. If the Earth doesn't address the growth and spread of its human infection, it may never recover.

My final analysis … I must not want my DNA to survive, because despite the sexually suggestive smile, and equally suggestive body language of Mary, I cannot find the slightest hint of motivation to do anything about it. I fully intend on going home alone tonight.

"You seem so distant. What's wrong?" It's an unusually alarming statement, as if Mary can read my mind.

"I don't feel any different than usual." I've got a lot on my mind and I can't shake this feeling that I should be somewhere else. Preferably alone. This must have something to do with the other night. I can't remember much, just arriving at the bar and sitting with Mary. After that, alcohol seems to have prevented the natural processes required to form a memory from forming. Alcohol has that effect on me … I drink so much and then suddenly I just wake up. I don't seem to have any self-control. I want to get away from my thoughts and blur the space between myself and others, so I drink until I'm gone. From what Jeff and Steve say, I turn into a likeable person when I drink too much.

"Excuse me for a minute. I need to use the head." Mary, Jeff, and Steve don't say anything, they just pass each other a poorly hidden series of glares. I'm trying not to notice, but it seems clear they are concerned about my wellbeing. I'm not sure how to relate and it makes feel uncomfortable with the situation. I can't quite breathe.

I stumble into the washroom, I haven't taken a breath since I left my table.
Inhale.
Exhale.

The sink is only a few steps away from the bathroom door. Above the dirty white porcelain sink is a mirror that stretches the length of the wall and reaches up to the ceiling. Talk about overkill. Looking into the mirror I try to recall the last time I smiled. Maybe I should try now. I always hear people going on about self-improvement and how they read articles in magazines to learn how to become more likeable. Standing upright, I force my lips to curve into the most unnatural smile imaginable. I hold the smile just long enough to cause the man exiting the stall behind to reconsider washing his hands in the sink beside me. I hope he didn't order nachos. After the stranger leaves the room, I put my smile away and reach out slowly to turn on the tap. Leaning over the sink I close my eyes, hold my hand out to the stream of water pouring from the tap, and start splashing water over my face erratically. It's irrational to think that washing my face with cold water will do anything to help my current situation, but I'm doing it anyway.

I've got both my hands on the sink to hold my weight as I lean forward. It appears that I'm at a crossroads. I can choose to go back out to the bar and spend the night with Jeff, Steve, and Mary, or I can bolt. I can find the nearest exit, slip out unnoticed, and go home where I'm comfortable and have no expectations to deal with. I don't need to try to be somebody. I can quietly be nothing.

I choose … alcohol. Drinking has always blurred my discomfort into something I can't even feel. Maybe I'm just an asshole when I'm sober, and I should spend more time intoxicated and accepting where I'm at in life. I towel off my face, find my resolve, and head out the door – carefully projecting as much confidence with my stride as I can. I am now in a live production and the audience is all around.

The man who didn't wash his hands is playing with the straw in his drink. He is literally about to drink his own shit next time he puts that straw in his mouth.

"Are you feeling OK?" Mary asks me as I sit down.

"Of course. Just a little stressed about keeping to my printing quota."

"I know, right? You see how we're only allowed one pen per month? Do you know how often I lose my pens? I swear someone in the office goes around at lunch stealing pens." Steve pounds his fist jokingly on the table.

Jeff points at Steve with his index finger. "You know who it is, don't you? It's probably Dave. He doesn't even eat lunch. He just walks around and steals our pens while we're eating. He probably has drawers full of our pens."

"Pretty smart move. He can start selling us our pens back when things get desperate." My comment is a hit, as everyone is now laughing. I nervously start taking large gulps of my beer.

"So what was up with you and Dave today, anyway? It's all anyone can chatter about." Steve cuts right to the chase. It almost feels like I was invited out just so they could get the inside scoop on the most eventful altercation in the office.

"I thought he wrote me a nasty note or something. Can we talk about something else?"

"Why would Dave write a nasty note? I could throw a coffee on him and he'd probably apologize to me for getting in the way." Mary seems to be pressing me to keep talking about Dave and his fucking note.

"I don't know. Do we need to talk about it?"

"No, I suppose not." Mary seems disappointed in my unwillingness to talk about my fight with Dave. Just once I wish they would talk about how they gagged when they peeled their banana and saw how mushy and bruised it was; instead, I am treated with inquisitive jabs into my personal life.

"What I want to talk about," Steve pauses for dramatic effect, "is how tight is too tight for dress pants. I feel I'm towing the line here with these fitted pants. They're wool, by the way. The real wool."

"As opposed to that fake wool?" Jeff snorts.

Mary slams her hand on the table in a polite gesture to gain the attention of the group. "You know, I saw a new guy walking down in the main lobby the other day. Young guy, real cute. Now *his* pants, his pants were too tight."

"Did you see an outline?" Steve leans closer to Mary, a little too eager for additional details it seems.

"Worse. I was walking behind him, and it's literally like some sort of force was sucking his pants into his asshole. I wanted to pick his wedgie for him. And to make it worse, his pant legs hovered at least four inches above his ankles."

Steve and Jeff are having a good laugh about the thought of some guy's flood pants. To take the pressure off the fact that I'm not laughing, I blurt out my best attempt at a joke.

"Well, Steve. Are your pants being forcefully sucked into your asshole? I guess that's the indicator if your pants are too tight."

"You know, I don't think I've reached that point yet."

What the hell are we even talking about, I wonder. Did Carl Sagan ever spend the night talking about whether his pants were too tight? Does a guy like that ever have a pointless conversation, or does everything always turn into a lesson on the inner workings of the universe? Carl Sagan would probably jump on the opportunity to compare pants being inhaled into a man's asshole to being sucked into a black hole.

Imagine Steve's pants represent a solar system. Each stride he takes moves him away from his point of origin, expanding outward like the stars into the gaping advance of space itself. At the centre of the solar system, his asshole acts like a black hole. It's expanding outward with his pants, but it's also absorbing all matter and energy around it with force. Does his asshole bend space and time? He'd probably follow up with some stellar insight into how a black hole may be a gateway to some alternate universe, represented through Steve's small intestine at the other end of the sphincter, and we'd all just lean on the table and listen intently.

If I were a smarter person, maybe people would spend more time listening to me and less time telling me about the phone conversation they had with their mom the other night.

Chapter 15

Two musclehead idiots are at the water cooler talking about how much they can bench press. Two large men, with what I am inferring to be latent homosexual urges, are showing each other how they perform a squat while holding a dumbbell in front of their chest. They are the kind of guys who spend most of their time at the gym coyly flexing in the mirror as if no one else can see them, as if their rituals of self-admiration were a discrete practice. They are not gay so much as they are narcissistic. They are gay for themselves. Most men struggle to keep their eyes away from a woman's cleavage at the gym, these men struggle to keep their eyes from ogling their own biceps.

I can see the blatant display of self-affection from the end of the hallway. It's amazing that neither of these men seems to be able to register that the affectionate way they undress themselves with their own eyes is not normal. They aren't even listening to each other. They are just engaged in a battle of self-aggrandizement that can only end when one of these two meat monkeys depletes his reserve of self-references.

"I use a straight bar, load it up with 350 pounds to build my glutes."

"One time I squatted 400 pounds, one rep, straight up with no spot."

I'd liken it to a penis measuring contest, but both these men are too wrapped up in their own self-admiration to care what the other person is holding in their hand. So, I guess it is a penis self-admiration contest.

Avoiding any sort of eye contact, I do my best to squeeze between these two large men and pour some water into my cup. I'm terrified I might become collateral damage during a demonstration of a squat. As the water pours into my cup I am struck by the image of an overdeveloped pair of glutes thrusting towards me as a wild squat goes rogue. I see myself flailing and fighting against the inevitable as I'm pushed up against the wall between muscular butt cheeks. I shudder at the thought of assuming the role of a hot dog in a bun and head back to my desk.

Flopping down into my chair I cross my arms and look around at the four walls that surround me. I'm drawn in by a picture nested on the cubicle wall adjacent to my desk. It's a picture of a small house on a very flat landscape. The house is plain, insignificant, and tucked away in the bottom corner of the photo. The house is overshadowed by an immense sky and horizon. The sky seems so big that it envelops the house and the small edge of land that appears in the bottom of the picture. This picture makes me feel small and constantly reminds me that depending on your perspective – the world can be an overwhelming place. Most people tell me that the photo is depressing, but I just think they fail to realize the beauty behind accepting the insignificance of our lives. No matter what mistakes we make, time and space will irrevocably erase any remnants of our actions. When faced with the enormity of the universe, one has to wonder why we place so much value on socks that match our pants and complement our shoes.

"Boy, I'd hate to live there."

I hadn't noticed Mr. Reid standing beside me. Apparently, he has been standing behind me and looking at the photo with me. I'm glad he hasn't taken it upon himself to ghost me like Patrick Swayze.

"Not much to look at other than the sky. Can't imagine what they'd do for fun out there."

"Maybe they'd enjoy some fresh air and exercise. It's an acquired taste." I look at Mr. Reid and smirk with my arms still crossed. Not the best body language to present your boss.

"Listen, I need to talk to you about something that happened the other day. Come see me in my office in an hour. This isn't an option." Reid doesn't even look at me, his eyes stay focused on the picture of the house hanging behind me. He lets out a sigh and quietly walks away. Something tells me that Reid might enjoy the freedom that solitude would offer him.

I can feel a shift in the atmosphere of the office. What Reid just said to me must have echoed throughout the office. I can feel its reverberations like when the air suddenly goes from hot to cold, and you become astutely aware of the overwhelming silence just before a tornado. Everyone in the office is fixated on me. They have sucked the compassion out of the room and turned the air cold. I can feel their judgmental gazes on me as they sit ready to pour out theories and accusations as soon as I leave the room. An outpouring of curiosity and speculation will collide with apprehension about my summoning, creating a downpour of gossip.

I wheel my chair in close to my desk and hunch down until I know I am completely out of everyone's sight. My cubicle provides me little comfort from the muffled whispers of the peanut gallery: the collective of office workers that have nothing better to do than complain about everyone around them. I do what I can to avoid being the main subject of office banter, but today I am unavoidably the topic of whispers.

The next hour seems to pass by at an alarming pace, which when I really think about it doesn't makes any sense. It takes an hour for an hour to pass. It can't be any longer or shorter, otherwise it would not be an hour. After the passing of a standard sixty-minute period, it's time for me to face the waiting eyes of my coworkers perched on the edges of their chairs, eager to catch a glance of my sluggish walk into Reid's office. I can only imagine the conversations everyone will have while I am locked up with Reid. Imaginations tend to run wild when you think the worst of someone, and since I've done little to endear myself to my colleagues, I can only assume they are thinking the worst of me.

I keep my head down but still try to exude confidence as I stroll towards Reid's door. The large black door that leads into Reid's office is closed and unwelcoming, but I knock anyway. Our office is too cheap to provide upper management like Reid his own personal secretary to act as a gatekeeper for his meetings, so he is completely responsible for arranging his own business ventures. The door opens slowly and Reid gestures for me to enter his room. His face is as solemn as I have ever seen it.

"Take a seat." Reid gestures to the only chair positioned across from his desk, a chair that I was already on my way to sit in. I suppose common sense had motivated me to sit in the only available chair in the room prior to Reid ever prompting me. It's not like I was going to sit on the floor, or put one foot in his trash can and stand there staring at him like an idiot. Telling me to sit in the chair is Reid's way of asserting dominance over me. Free will does not direct me to sit in his chair, I merely obey Reid's direction.

"You've been with us for a while now, and we haven't had any issues with your performance or conduct. That's why I find your altercation with Dave the other day so alarming. I actually received numerous complaints and concerns about your behaviour that day, and frankly this worries me."

Silence. Reid's eyes are fixated on me, and it's clear he is contemplating what to say next. "I am recommending you see a counsellor. It's the kind of recommendation that if you don't follow, you likely won't be employed here much longer."

"Counselling?"

"Yes. The office has a counsellor on retainer to help employees deal with stress, depression ... all sorts of issues. It's covered by your benefits, so you don't have to worry about affording it. All you need to do is show up, and make sure there is no repeat behaviour."

"So, you're forcing me to attend counselling to keep my job?"

"Well, if you don't attend, I can't guarantee that we can continue to employ you. If you don't want to make the effort to keep your job, then we won't make the effort on your behalf."

I can sense an understanding between Reid and myself. I don't verbalize it, but we both know where I stand.

"And so how do I arrange a meeting with this counsellor?"

"I see you aren't familiar with our employee assistance program." Reid reaches down into his bottom drawer and pulls out a colourful pamphlet. "Take this pamphlet. Inside is all the information you need about our insurance provider options. If you have any questions, direct those to human resources. There's a number in the pamphlet."

Reid leans back into his chair. It seems he is finished talking, though he hasn't used any of the traditional methods for communicating that a conversation has come to a close. I purse my lips, nod my head, and stand up. Reid doesn't provide me with the customary reciprocation of my ascent from the chair. I find this to be a curious move: either he doesn't respect me, or he is trying to intimidate me. Either way, I choose to not extend my hand. Instead, I look Reid in the eye and thrust my hands into my pockets in an exaggerated motion. I smile and leave the room, hoping to have regained a morsel of power by burying my hands in my pockets. No more words need to be exchanged between us. I understand where I've gone wrong, and now I must do my penance. I've made myself stand out, and not in a positive way. I've put so much effort into going unnoticed that this recent development is really quite off-putting for me.

If Dave really had planted the note to sabotage my focus in my recent presentation, then he has gotten more than he could have ever bargained for. He's goaded me into a public outburst that has effectively ostracized me from my colleagues and labelled me as a deviant with my boss. Fortunately, if I am compliant with the recommended rehabilitation, I cannot be dismissed. Dave's move will backfire as long as I am cooperative. Funny, it never occurred to me before that by acting crazy I could provide myself with the type of job security that hard work never could. Employers are too worried about potential lawsuits that might occur if they were to fire someone with an identified mental health condition. Entire organizations have cropped up with the specific goal of defending employees who are undergoing treatment for a variety of mental health concerns. Hardworking employees like Dave are out of luck because they are too honest to ever admit their stress is a debilitating condition. Nobody would ever believe them if they did; they are just too productive.

The office has turned on me and will view me with wariness until I can regain their trust and fit in again. Trust is just a way to describe an absence of anxiety caused by my presence. Right now, I am so unpredictable and frightening, I might just snatch the pen out of someone's hands and snap it in half right before their eyes. My presence creates a heightened sense of anxiety to anyone within an arm's length of me. They just can't be sure whether or not I will touch something of theirs. I am able to infer this as I travel the walk of shame from Reid's office by the not-so subtle way everyone pulls their office supplies closer to their bodies and avoids looking at me. I'm fairly certain that Jeff will soon find his way into my workspace and casually interrogate me for information.

Jeff is right on cue. As I take my seat and assume the standard working position, Jeff casually takes up a lean at the entrance to my workspace.

"So, got called to the gallows, eh?"

"You could say that, Jeff. I'm not too worried about it."

Jeff tries to read my eyes to really gauge how I feel, but I am in control of my emotions. Jeff will get nothing.

"Is this about your meltdown with Dave the other day? What the hell happened, anyway? I've heard like six different stories about it."

"Eye witness accounts have time and time again proven to be rife with inaccuracies. When people replay an event in their head, they often add details congruent with their personal biases."

"Well, that's a veiled answer if I've ever heard it." Jeff sounds unimpressed with me. "What really happened?"

"Not that it's any of your business, but I have reason to believe Dave left a threatening note on my desk. I confronted him about it, and he played dumb."

"Why would the Slave leave a threatening note? I don't even think he'd threaten a mosquito that's biting him. He'd just keep trying to ask it if there was some way he could help. He's a total wuss." Jeff seems curiously defensive about Dave.

"I've got a few reasons. Steve and I were about to do an important presentation that day, on the same day as Dave. Rumour is the presentation would determine who would remain employed. Dave knows he'd lose his job if it came down to a popularity contest, so he tried to throw us off."

"That's quite the story." Jeff starts searching my desk with his eyes. "You got the note?"

"No, can't remember what I did with it."

"Listen, I wouldn't worry about it. Probably just some prank that someone forgot to tell you about. And I highly doubt it was Dave. You should probably just let it go."

"Yah." I smile, processing what Jeff has just said. "You're probably right." Maybe it wasn't Dave.

Why would Jeff try to convince me it was just a practical joke that someone forgot to admit to? It seems like Jeff might have just ousted himself in an attempt to prevent his lark from spiralling any more out of control. Jeff is popular enough to know that his tomfoolery temporarily provides others with a feeling of being accepted. He exudes cool and all anyone wants is to be included in anything he does.

My predicament is the result of a joke. Not the first time this thought has crossed my mind.

Chapter 16

4:00 pm. I've reached the point in my day where I couldn't care less about starting a new task or completing the one I am currently working on. After all, if I were to keep working, how much further ahead would I be at the end of the day? Only thirty minutes, and thirty minutes is a small enough window for me to not care. There are a few ways I prefer to spend my last half hour at work: I either sit at my computer and just open and close folders on my screen repetitively, or I look for objects I can innocuously place disparaging words onto. Over the past few weeks I've slowly hidden disparaging words throughout the office, and not a single word or phrase has been removed. I'm convinced that people in the office are not paying attention to their surroundings. I don't even find it funny anymore. Instead, placing disparaging words around the office has become a game. I feed off the exhilaration of being caught and become slightly bolder in my placement. If a person were to notice just one word, then in accordance with the domino effect, every other word I've hidden will suddenly become illuminated. It will be like a grand awakening, only instead of reaching enlightenment my coworkers will reach new levels of mistrust.

Today I used my label maker to print the words "Give Up." I have a small glimmer of hope that my coworkers are subconsciously internalizing the messages that I am leaving for them and that my disparaging words hidden throughout the office make everyone feel uneasy about their lives. I don't feel badly about making others feel discontent. I've read many times before that satisfaction or contentment with life leads to a decline in ambition, but dissatisfaction with life can motivate a person to take action and be ambitious. You can't want to work hard to improve your life if you don't hate it, so enough with unconditionally loving yourself. People need to hate something about their lives enough to want to make it better. So, I am really just trying to motivate my colleagues to find a better career, or seek personal improvement by creating widespread dissatisfaction about their current self-concept.

"You're not sexually appealing" hidden at the back of the cupboard in the office kitchen. A call to spend more time taking care of one's physical appearance. Maybe exercise more, try a new hairstyle, or iron your shirt.

"No one loves you" stuck on the inside lip of the elevator. A plea to work harder at developing deeper connections with the people around you.

"Dumb bastard" carefully placed on the inside of Reid's door frame. A commentary on how someone's ignorance towards their intellectual limitations can have a profound impact on the people around them.

My target today will likely be the inside lid of the staff photocopier. The photocopier is probably the most used machine in the office and yet I can't imagine anyone will notice the small black letters printed on a white label, stuck right in plain sight. Perhaps the best part about hiding a word on the inner lid of the photocopier is that every page the photocopier will produce through the scan function will bear the faint shadow of the words *give up*. The paper we use is not thin enough for the word to seep completely through the backside of the paper, so the word will only appear as a faint discolouration and will unfortunately be mirrored. I hear the subconscious is pretty good at deciphering subliminal messages, even if they are written backwards, so I am confident that my co-workers' satisfaction will slowly disintegrate with each photocopy they make.

I'm not the first person to realize that people don't pay attention at work. I'm just following the footsteps of Tom Moore Jr., a member of the Texas State House. Tom got tired of everyone just going through the motions and passing bills blindly because the title sounded good. Knowing that everyone he worked with ignored their straightforward job of reading carefully with concern for consequences, Tom put forward a bill to be passed through legislation that would make everyone look like an idiot. Clear as day, the bill recommended that the city honour the Boston Strangler as a humanitarian, devoted to helping solve the world's over-population problem. The bill passed without question, confirming Tom's notion that his colleagues do not pay attention to the words in front of them, and making everyone in the House look like an idiot to all their constituents.

The first sticky label I put up in the office said "Enter to die a little bit more each day." It's located right underneath the company logo that hangs above the main entrance. I don't imagine many people think to look up before passing through the door, but something about posting an unseen message to my colleagues exhilarates me. It's not as significant a victory as having a bill passed through a State House, but I still take pride in my small victory. Eventually I might become bold enough to start labelling the insides of people's cubicles. I could stick a label that says, "you're trapped" in the far corner of someone's desk, right where the desk meets the cubicle wall at a ninety-degree angle.

The most difficult part about labelling the office with disparaging notes is keeping your actions discrete. I grab the label maker from the drawer and thumb the appropriate keys. I make sure to select size six font. I'm bold, but I'm not size twelve bold. I have to be prepared for the fact that someone will probably stop me to ask what I'm doing. As soon as I tell them I am going to photocopy something, I'm sure they'll ask,

"Oh, well what are ya' making copies of?"

My response likely doesn't matter. I could probably say, "Pornographic images. I just have the sudden urge to decorate my cubicle with something a little more erotic."

And the person will just nod their head and reply, "Totally. Well, have a good one!"

I grab the small label I just printed and a random budget breakdown before making my way to the photocopier. My first few steps look promising: the office is quiet and there is not a coworker in sight. I glance at the watch on my wrist and see it's 4:22 pm. With eight minutes left in the workday most people are probably just waiting patiently at their desks until they are allowed to leave. Arriving at the photocopier I casually lift the lid and place the budget down. I choose to position myself in a comfortable looking side lean, the kind where you lean on one arm and shift the weight in your feet to raise one butt cheek slightly – sort of like the way Spock would raise his eyebrows when fascinated. I make sure to look in both directions before placing the label on the top of the machine lid, and see that there's still not a person in view. Misbehaviour doesn't have the same appeal without the danger of being caught. I wait around the photocopier for two or three more minutes, just holding the budget down against the glass of the copier until the presence of someone else necessitates that I move.

"Are you going to use the machine? I'd like to copy these before I go home."

I look up and see an irritated-looking Dave standing to my left. He must have quiet shoes. First, he walks out of the office conference room without anyone noticing, and now he sneaks up behind me at the photocopier without the typical clomp of dress shoes. Formal footwear often results in a trotting sound, not unlike the band of iron nailed to the bottom of a horse's hoof, but Dave's shoes fall silently to the ground.

"Sorry. I must be daydreaming." I pull the paper off the machine and start to walk away, avoiding any kind of eye contact with Dave. Maybe this is the moment. The office has been unusually silent the past few minutes with no keyboards clicking, no muffled laughs off in the distance – just silence. Maybe Dave killed everyone, and he's here to deliver on his promise of killing me last.

"Hey," Dave's voice is calm, but there is a hint of angst. I stop walking and turn to face Dave. I'm quickly relived to see that Dave is not brandishing a gun, but only pointing at the photocopier.

"You never photocopied anything."

"Changed my mind." If Dave didn't write that note, he must think I've completely lost my mind. I raise my arm to look at my watch: It's 4:27 pm.

If I could think about the world in a different way, would I be a happier person?

Chapter 17

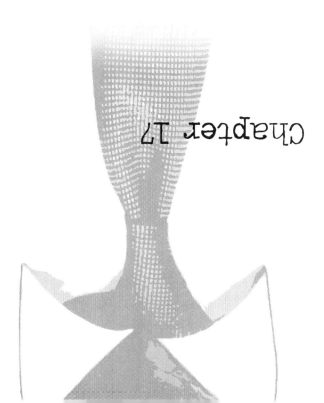

We are terrified of being alone. We may say we fear being unwanted or unloved, but that is just a narrative spun in our heads because the world has told us that we ought to feel sad and discontent if we are alone. The prevailing attitude is that we are not normal if we choose to be alone. I must be the only person who realizes that the reason the world is full of depressed, miserable assholes is because we are pressured into relationships and obligation. Instead of finding someone who truly complements us, we learn to settle for the first person who will reciprocate our complacency. We ought to find more time to spend alone learning to be comfortable with ourselves. Too much time is spent chasing after the approval of others and ignoring the fact that we were meant to be the whole on our own.

I only feel at ease when my obligation to others is absent. My work-centered lifestyle has created a deeply repressed fantasy to explore the world with no strings attached. Imagine, travelling without worrying about work, bills, relationships, and other responsibilities. No distraction.

To a counsellor, these are not normal thought processes and likely set off an internal alarm. *Anxious loner alert.* My office-appointed counsellor is an older man. He has a gentle, grandfatherly aura about him, although he

doesn't have much of a counsellor name. Tim. What kind of name is Tim? I can only assume Tim is thinking that I am making a concerted effort to avoid addressing my emotions by providing an intellectualized rationale for why I dislike people. He feels he will break down my intellectual walls and find the emotions buried deep within. Deep down, he is going to find the fuzzy teddy bear who just wants a hug and to be liked by his peers.

"You don't sound happy."

"Very astute, Tim."

There is a long silence survived by an intense period of uninterrupted eye contact. Tim blinks first. My silent hostility must be sparking Tim's curiosity. *Have I hit a nerve? Should I break the silence, or should I refuse to back down from this game of verbal chicken?*

"You feel like you have too many obligations and you don't have time for yourself. You're concerned about making the wrong career or relationship choice, and what the wrong choice might mean for you." Tim must be proud of this statement. I can sense the pride behind his words expressed through the subtle smile and glint in his eyes.

"I'm more concerned that I am going to have to spend the rest of my life doing what other people tell me to do. I'm concerned that there is no room left in the world for creativity. School and work have beat dreams and creativity out of us with routine, tedium, and ever-growing responsibility. We're just chasing the dollar now, dreaming about finally retiring and ending the cycle of obligation. We are what school has made us settle for being and we've been convinced it was our dream all along." I find myself out of breath, as if I just sprinted up a stair case.

"It sounds like you've thought about this a lot. You have quite the story worked out. Seems life isn't the way you thought it would be. You want more choice. A greater sense of freedom.

"That is the most sensible thing you've said all day, Tim. Maybe you're not so bad after all. Be honest: don't you just want to tell your clients to shut the fuck up? You can't honestly tell me you care what we have to say. You are here because you needed to find something that would pay you enough money to survive comfortably."

"If that's how you want to look at it. It sounds like you've already made up your mind about my motives, so I can't see what good it will do to convince you otherwise. I do care, and it does make me feel good that I can help others."

"Sounds more like it makes you feel good to solve people. Like a puzzle, people present you with a challenge, and solving the puzzle makes you feel smart."

"And you find the thought of me potentially getting a sense of personal satisfaction to be … the wrong type of motivation?"

"I don't know. You tell me. Are you in it for your own personal satisfaction, or are you in it because you selflessly want to better the lives of your clients?"

I can see Tim studying my face. He seems to be impossible to bring to anger and remains calm and collected despite my challenges to his motivation.

"You don't seem to believe that people are capable of helping someone for the sake of helping."

"No. People will only help someone if they stand to gain from it. If everyone went out of their way to raise the quality of life of the people around them, then I don't imagine our world would look as shitty as it does."

"You're pretty convinced that the world is laden with ill intention. You don't think people are capable of caring for each other. One thing I would be interested in hearing is more about how you feel. I've heard a lot of what you think, but nothing about what you feel. We don't have too much time left here today, but this has been an interesting conversation." Tim casually lifts his right leg, and crosses it over his left. His elbows rest on his thigh, supporting the weight of his large head. "I'd like to get deeper into it next week. Consider how all of this makes you feel. Take some time. We'll talk about it next week."

Tim smiles and looks almost relieved for this conversation to be over. As a professional Tim must be aware that no behavioural issue or emotional state can be altered or *fixed* in a matter of hours. Fixed implies that someone's personality is broken, but how are we supposed to know what the personality was before it broke? Maybe some personalities are just made wrong at the factory.

"So … this is the end of the session?" I'm practically taunting Tim with my tone and closed body language.

"Yes. We're drawing to a close. How did it feel for you?"

With a snort, I let Tim have it. "Pretty useless. Like a waste of time."

Nodding, Tim starts rubbing his chin. "I'd agree. It was a pretty big waste of time." Tim notices the shock on my face, in a way it feels like I've just been slapped. "You seem surprised that I agree."

"Well – yes … I …" I'm at a loss for words.

Tim uncrosses his legs and tilts his head slightly to the side. There's a softness to his eyes as he looks good and hard at me. "You know, counselling requires that you do a lot of work. Uncomfortable work. Today was a waste of time, because you don't come across as interested in doing any work – in being uncomfortable. It feels to me that you are quite firm about not needing to change. There's an anger underneath it all, maybe you find yourself resenting being here."

I'm nodding my head. My heart is pounding. There's an unwanted build up of moisture in my eyes. Who knew words had so much power? Tim is calling me out, and yet I find myself distraught.

"There may be some resentment about being here."

"You don't feel you need to be here."

"That's right."

"Hm." Tim is quick to pounce. "So, you aren't happy. And you don't feel there is any reason to be here."

"That's right." I lift my chin to signal that I'm still up for a fight."

"You seem to take pride in that."

Maybe I'm not ready for this fight. "What?" Is all I manage as a counter.

"I can respect that you don't want to be here. You were forced here, if I'm not mistaken, by work. I find it odd though, that you seem to take pride in being unhappy."

"Would you prefer I was happy?" I'm trying to mock Tim and his happiness fetish.

"How would your life be different if you did?"

Tim is a heavy hitter. I don't even want to fight anymore.

"We have several weeks together." Tim's body seems to deflate as he relaxes. "Let's make this time worthwhile, for both of us. You asked me if I would prefer if you were happy. I'd prefer if you would make an honest effort to explore your feelings. Throughout this conversation, I've sensed a lot of emotion – but only heard thoughts and rationalizations. Perhaps this is something we can work on. And whether or not you want to be happy, I'll leave for you to figure out."

Fuck.

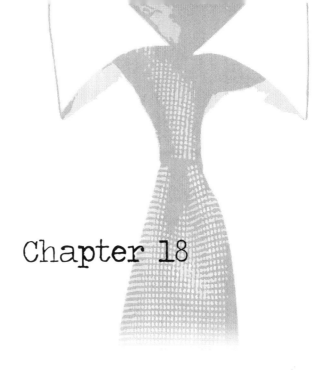

Chapter 18

I'm at my desk again. Or maybe I never left. Work days have a monotonous way of blending into each other with nothing ever really standing out. Same scenery, same people, same issues, and same tasks. Tuesday's crisis is revisited the following week on a Thursday, and Wednesday's phone call seems to be reenacted on Monday with another player. I might have just talked to Steve about our recent presentation, but that might have happened last week. I can't really tell anymore. I am constantly repeating the same tasks and dealing with the same idiots at work causing the same problems. Despite our unique ability to communicate and learn from each other's mistakes, most humans can't be bothered to pay attention. And don't bother trying to tell someone what is best for them, that will just reinforce their desire to do the opposite. Most people will endure any hardship to avoid the embarrassment of accepting they are wrong.

So when Marty, the guy inhabiting the cubicle beside me, asks me to turn down the music playing on my computer because it is disrupting his work environment, naturally I resist. Mark Knopfler's iconic guitar riff was meant to be loud, and I'd prefer to not insult Mark, so I grab hold of my keyboard and repeatedly smash the little plus symbol to bring Marty into dire straits.

"that ain't workin' that's the way you do it. Money for nothin' and chicks for free."

I can hear Marty mutter something, but I can't tell what. My music is much too loud for me to hear what anyone outside of my cubicle is saying.

"We gotta install microwave ovens. Custom kitchen deliveries"

This might be the most relaxed I've ever been at work. Peeking over the top of my cubicle, Marty shouts at me, "Can you put in some earphones?"

"Don't want your MTV?" I laugh.

Marty pushes off the cubicle wall and stomps his way around to my entrance, anger expressed in the intensity of each step. If intimidating me was the goal of walking like an upset toddler, Marty may need to fall back on plugging his ears and screaming.

"You are being really disruptive." Marty is now in my cubicle. He is physically in my cubicle and he is completely unwelcome.

"Marty, if you really wanted to get your work done, I doubt a little music would keep you from it. See, I think you really don't want to work, and you're using this situation to justify your lack of productivity. So why don't you trot on back to your desk, and quit blaming me for your poor motivation and work habits." I try to shoo Marty away with a dismissive flick of my wrist.

"I tried to ask nicely, but now I'm going to have to tell Reid." Marty just threatened to tattle. He totally skipped sticking his fingers in his ears and instead went straight to yelling for Mom and Dad to intervene. It's clear Marty is aggravated, but a lifetime of being told to play nice, be quiet, and behave has effectively castrated Marty's ability to properly stand up for himself. Marty's only recourse is to file a complaint with my boss and go back and sit at his desk quietly, satisfied that he did the right thing.

I don't imagine my latest outburst will go over well with Reid. I'm in counselling, so my disruptive behaviour can be explained away by the emotional difficulties I've been directed to resolve through professional services. The only action Reid can take is asking me to take time off from work, but Reid is savvy enough to know that time off is no real punishment for a person like me. My absence will do nothing but disturb everyone around me. Like a giant flare, my absence will be immediately noticed by everyone in the office and will dominate lunch time conversation. While the office falls into gossip-fueled disarray, I will be enjoying personal freedom: a paycheck without the cumbersome demands of a work week.

I think I'll keep my music playing loudly until lunch. It is about an hour away, and it will give everyone something to talk about while I bruise their bananas and add salt to their coffee cream. Strange how being loud and obnoxious can sometimes make people ignore you. Being obnoxious may even keep me from being invited out again. Jeff and Mary likely want to avoid staining their social resumes by hanging out with the office crazy.

I put my hands behind my head, lean back into my chair, and rock back and forth like an old, relaxed man in his favourite rocker. My brief moment of satisfaction is strangled by the nagging whine of my phone. As a kid, phone calls used to excite me, but now, as a full time employee, a phone call does nothing but make me feel sick. I pick up the phone and instantly recognize the voice on the other line. No doubt Marty has turned me in to the authorities for unnecessary enjoyment of my day and they mean to throw the book at me. Reid has asked me to join him upstairs on the fifth floor where the human resource department is located. Nothing good can come from a trip upstairs. No doubt Marty's phone call is what prompted Reid to send me upstairs, so in the spirit of the Code of Hammurabi, I'm going to return Marty's slight with a slight of my own. Marty is the kind of guy who neurotically labels every item in his lunch just to make sure no one accidently eats his food. I grab my stapler and squeeze off one into my hand before leaving my cubicle for the kitchen. I intend to cause mischief. Walking along the outside of the office walls to avoid garnering too much attention, I start bending the staple into a straight line.

Skimming through the fridge in the office kitchen, I find a large red lunch pail labelled *Martin deVries*. Unzipping his lunch pail, I reach in and grab what feels to be an apple. Pulling my arm back out of the lunch pail with Marty's apple I can see a piece of brown tape with his name written in black marker. How he has time to label his fruit in the morning is beyond me. Using the straightened staple, I start poking small, deep holes over as much of the apple's surface as possible. In a few hours his apple will be dried out and the texture of the rotted apple will hopefully cause Marty to gag. Next I grab a plastic container with some sort of pasta in a white cream sauce. I pop the lid off and pour some of the vinegar I took from the side shelf into the pasta container. I want to be sure it mixes well, so I put the lid back on and shake up the pasta as violently as I can. All I can think about while I'm shaking his pasta is that scene in Star Wars where Chewbacca is strangling Lando. *We understand, don't we Chewy. You had no choice*, I whisper in an angry tone, shaking the plastic container harder as each word comes out. The last blow I decide to strike is to eat Marty's chocolate chip cookies. The Ziploc bag is clearly labelled *Marty*, but the contents of this particular resealable plastic bag will never make it into the hands of Marty. He will not know the pleasure of his cookies today. Shutting the fridge door, I can't help but notice the homemade quality of his cookies. They are soft, with a hint of crunch from crushed up nuts mixed right into the batter – clearly not store-bought.

I decide I should take the elevator to the fifth floor today. As much as I prefer the quiet of the stairwell, I don't want to be sweaty and out of breath when I arrive at my meeting. If I'm lucky, no one will be in the elevator with me … I might even have the freedom to pass gas. When the door opens I am disappointed to see a large crowd of people packed into the elevator and the lights on the panel are lit up all the way from the second floor to the fifth. This is going to be a long ride and I just finished my last cookie.

It never fails. Put a group of strangers in a small space like an elevator for an extended period of time and everyone will become noticeably uncomfortable. It's only a matter of time before one person will decide to take the initiative to announce something obvious. They will spend minutes gathering the strength and courage from the awkward silence to break the unstated desire of the other occupants, *just keep to yourself.* I can see today's martyr in the elevator surveying the audience, her eyes methodically roaming from person to person looking for any kind of incidental eye contact. Her hands are grasping the handles of her purse and she is shifting the weight of her body from hip to hip, so casual and cool. As soon as someone makes the mistake of returning her stare, she will seize the opportunity to blurt out an obvious statement.

"Gee, this elevator sure is moving slow, am I right!?" The martyr's mouth forms a gaping hole as she laughs nervously in anticipation of someone validating her perceptive comment.

"You bet," announces another dunce. This person has been waiting patiently to leach onto any comment with an affirming statement. He has no opinion or thoughts of his own, only a deep-seated desire to be accepted by this group of strangers. His enthusiastic agreement, always in four words or less, is a reflexive response developed through years of agreeing. Any conflicting statement made by a group member can cause an internal struggle: *I already agreed to the first person; agreeing with the second person means I now disagree with the first person. Since I already agreed, I can't now disagree, how can I agree with both …*

"I am just so ready for the weekend!" The martyr introduces a new insightful topic for the group to mull over.

"Can't come soon enough!" chirps the dunce in response, slapping his knee and releasing a gasp of excitement.

To send the dunce into a state of confusion, I announce my unease about the coming weekend. Silence overtakes the elevator as the dunce works out how to approach the conflicting statement in four words or less. I see the martyr make eye contact with him, smiling and bobbing her head as if she were cheering the dunce on. Energized by the support of his new-found fan, he manages to stumble out some words in cheerful prose.

"Oh, I've been there!" I can feel a hand gently grasp my right shoulder. As if talking to me wasn't enough, he also had to touch me. Sometimes I wish people would simply stand in silence and respect my desire to keep to myself. This is my punishment for trying to avoid physical exertion. Several seconds pass and the hand remains draped over my shoulder, soaking unwanted sweat and companionship into my shirt. I look at the hand and then edge my eyes up towards its owner in a concerted effort to send a message telepathically.

Get your fucking hand off my shoulder, I shout in my mind at the man. The message must have been received because the hand is now off my shoulder and there is a timid-looking man across from me. He reached out looking for acceptance but was met with disapproval.

Finally the elevator arrives at my floor, allowing me to leave these people behind forever. A rush of fresh air blasts me in the face as I step out of the elevator. I would say it's invigorating, but recycled air just doesn't seem to liven me up.

"Jackass." The words hit me in the back of the head after the elevator door shuts in the offbeat way that elevator doors do. Apparently an elevator is not soundproof, probably to allow any trapped occupant the opportunity to scream for help (or in my case, a dejected person to sound off their disapproval from the safety of a closed door).

I've departed the elevator with feedback, do I trust these strangers' assessment of me? Wrestling with how my behaviour has made me feel, I proceed down the corridor to my destination with the best mask I can generate on the fly. I am on the floor where all the human resource personnel are stowed away and intentionally isolated from the rest of the office. There is a mythos about human resources that is passed down through generations of office employees. They are not like regular employees: they don't feel compassion, harbour hate, or express joy. They lurk unseen in the shadows, listening for inappropriate comments and watching for any act that might be considered a form of sexual harassment. They carefully transform your behaviour, failures, and achievements into voodoo dossiers that inflict pain, decide worth in salary, and control your movement through the company. Human resource personnel are patient: they will wait months, sometimes years, before they call you to answer for a mistake you've made. You don't get called to this floor for friendly banter. I have been summoned to atone for my sins.

At the end of the corridor I can see my destination, Helen Killjoy's office. Helen's last name makes her even more intimidating than her power suit with padded shoulders already does. It's well-known that Helen Killjoy is responsible for enacting disciplinary measures and her name has been mentioned in many tales told around the staff lunchroom. Just whisper *Killjoy*, and watch as people in the office shudder. I've heard so many conflicting descriptions of what Helen Killjoy looks like. I've heard her described as freakishly tall, with shoulders as wide as an oven, a muscular jawline, and perfect skin void of any wrinkles. Another rumour is that Helen looks like a bitch.

Peering into Helen's office, I receive my first visual confirmation that she definitely has thick shoulder pads packed into her blazer. It's possible Helen has had to tackle employees who have run from her office, so the shoulder pads are likely a functional feature of her dress attire. In a chair just to the left of Helen's desk I can see Reid. Despite his manager status, Reid is positioned quite nominally in relation to Helen: he is exposed on the periphery of her desk and forced to lean uncomfortably against the outer edge. It's apparent that even Reid is wary of Helen Killjoy and his power is meaningless in her office.

"Please take a seat." Helen motions towards a chair with a nod of her head. I'm seven years old and in the principal's office.

"You've recently displayed some concerning behaviour. It is my understanding that you are currently in counselling to help manage your recent behaviour. I have recommended that you take the next two weeks off, and Mr. Reid here agrees."

"Two weeks?" Slouching into my chair, I find I'm not as happy to be given time off as I thought I'd be.

"Yes." Helen folds her hands on her desk. "We'd like you to take a break from work, collect yourself, and seek appropriate support so that you can return to work well." Helen opens the only file visible on her neatly kept desk, sifts through some papers, and removes a single piece of paper before closing the file. She takes her time reviewing whatever is written on the paper before putting it back on the desk. It is clear that she is in total control of the room. I can see Reid shift anxiously in the silence, but Helen Killjoy remains stoic and firm.

"It has also been recommended by your counsellor that you visit your family doctor for examination."

Cutting Helen off, I mutter, "I don't have a family doctor."

"A general practitioner will do. We want to ensure your overall physical wellbeing." Reid nods his head in solidarity with Helen's words, causing me to cock my head slightly as I question his motives.

"And if I am unable to get an appointment in the next two weeks?"

"Oh, don't worry." Helen smiles. "We can ensure an appointment is arranged in a timely manner."

"We'll need to know what the doctors say." Reid finally musters the strength to enter the conversation. Unfortunately, his contributions have only drawn the ire of Helen. Without breaking eye contact with me, Helen sternly addresses Reid.

"We are only required to know if there are any concerns relating to your ability to perform your work. We have a process to guide us across that bridge if it comes to that." Smiling, Helen punctuates the end of her sentence with a shift of her eyes in Reid's direction.

"I see. So what is my next step?"

Helen lifts the file on her desk and gives its spine a good tap against her table top. "Speak with Clarice on your way out. She will help you sort out the details. Your leave is to begin immediately. We will check in when you return and determine if you are capable of resuming duties."

Judgment has been passed.

Chapter 19

Everyone is on drugs. Prescription pills. Vitamins. Steroids. Energy boosters. Doesn't matter whether it's food or drink, everything seems to contain some sort of drug. Entire industries dependent on drugging the populace cropped up during the twentieth century. What role does our habitual doped-up state play in the constant struggle to deal with our thoughts? How is our motivation or our fear affected by the innocuous consumption of drugs that goes unquestioned? In an era of unparalleled standards of living and opportunity, people struggle to comprehend why they feel perpetually restless and despondant. Is it possible the human race is slowly losing clarity on reality? Of course, that is assuming humans have ever had the luxury of clarity. If anything, our perception of the external stimulus that informs reality has been nothing but muddied since we invented language to articulate our thoughts. We try to make a convincing argument that reality can be defined, but we invented the words we are trying to define it with. We seem to be stuck on the notion of a one-size-fits-all reality. Life is a shared experience, and we must all experience it the same way; otherwise we are weird and insane.

I am called by a nurse to transition from the waiting room to a smaller room comprised of an examination bed, a table, and a chair. The nurse hands me a clipboard and asks me to take a seat. Smiling politely she requests that I fill out the assessment forms on the clipboard and wait patiently for the next available doctor. Apparently, the doctor's diagnosis is dependent on my ability to check the appropriate boxes on the form. A scantron would likely be able to provide me with a similar diagnosis. Perhaps hospitals are shifting towards robotic doctors. Input the data, out comes the diagnosis and treatment.

I feel discouraged a lot.

I blow up easily.

I spend little time with friends.

I often don't feel like eating.

The first page seems to go on and on, listing statements and asking me to rate how representative of me the statements are. It seems strange that the questions are all worded so negatively. The form assumes that I am depressed, and it is trying to ascertain to what degree.

The second page bears a striking resemblance to Mad Libs. Instead of inserting humorous verbs I am asked to fill in my personal biography. Age, history of illness, marital status, history of jobs, and so on. I will be impressed if the doctor actually reads every last line I fill out on these forms. Somehow I doubt that will happen.

The third page lists a series of illnesses that I may have had in the past or that may run in the family. I am to check the corresponding box beside any illness that I've had. I could lie, just to see the initial shock on the doctor's face. *Let's see here, looks like you've recently had an eating disorder, drug addiction problem, fungal infections, lymphoma, herpes, abnormal sweating, rectal pain, and seizures. Have you been taking any medication?*

The form is unending. Page after page require details about my family history, symptoms, depressing thoughts that might have occurred to me, and feelings I have on a regular basis. List after list, check box after check box. I'm reminded of a sterilization program implemented at a prison camp in Nazi Germany. People considered unfit for breeding were asked to sit in an ordinary-looking waiting room. They were provided some forms and asked to fill them out, nothing out of the ordinary and no reason for the person to panic. The radiation that flooded the room had no scent, no colour, and no way of being detected. The person would spend an hour or more in the room, quietly filling out the requested forms and just soaking in dangerous amounts of radiation. Once the forms were filled out, the person was effectively sterile.

The radiation silently killed any chance the person had of reproducing, and the person would never know what really happened. Maybe the room I'm sitting in is flooded with low levels of radiation intended to prevent me from breeding.

Almost a full hour passes before I finally finish filling out the forms provided to me. I throw the clipboard to the side of the examination bed and rub my eyes. Right on cue, the nurse returns to the room to pick up the forms. She smiles politely but doesn't say anything before she leaves. I can only imagine the amount of upset patients that scream at her on a daily basis. Waiting seems to cause irrational people to yell at strangers. It's a mistake to think yelling can make anyone care about helping you solve your problem.

After a significant amount of time spent waiting on the examination bed, the doctor finally arrives. She enters the room while holding my file in front of her face and slowly walks towards the vacant chair, skipping any sort of introduction or pleasantry with me. In many ways she reminds me of a robot by the way she enters the room with perfect, upright posture. She seems to walk in straight lines and her entire upper body seems stiff as if some sort of frame is holding up her spine. As she takes her seat she doesn't slouch, but continues to remain upright and expressionless. She slowly puts the folder down into her lap and cocks her side slightly to the side.

"So what brings you here today." The doctor slowly tilts her head back into a rigid and streamlined position. Her voice is monotone and it almost seems as if she is making a statement rather than asking a question – as if she already has what she needs to know about me from my forms.

"Well, I was told by my work to see a doctor, make sure I'm healthy. I've been told to take a few weeks off, see a counsellor."

"I see. Have you been feeling depressed or anxious lately? Have you experienced any loss of sleep or appetite?" The doctor doesn't even have a pen in her hand, she is just sitting with her arms crossed over her lap. I give her a curious look, as I'm sure she must have already read the answers to those questions.

"Well, I guess you can say I experience anxiety about going to work. Something about knowing I'm going to spend the next forty years there just makes me anxious, call me crazy."

"Any loss of sleep?"

"No, if anything I'm sleeping more."

"I see." The doctor reaches for a pen from the front breast pocket of her coat and takes out a pad of paper from the desk drawer in front of her. She clicks her pen a few times and scribbles erratically on the pad of paper.

"According to your statements, you feel anxious at work."

The doctor looks up at me. Maybe this is another one of her questions pronounced as a statement.

"Yes. I feel anxious at work. Sometimes, I just sit in my chair and struggle to breathe. I get tense."

"Stress?" The doctor finally intonates her voice upwards to signal a question is being asked. I'll let go the absence of words in her query.

"Yes. I feel stress. It's like, I don't really know how to describe it. It's not really a headache. It's not overactive thoughts. It's like being underwater. I can sort of hear everything, there is a lot of pressure on me, I'm floating, struggling to breath, and I don't know – out of my element."

"I see." The doctor clicks her pen a few more times and starts to scribble a note. "Do you feel this way outside of work?"

"Outside of work, I feel relaxed."

"I see." The doctor scribbles another note, but this time she seems to pause. She is still pressing the pen against the paper. "What is it about being outside of work that makes you feel relaxed? Is it your partner, friends, a pet?"

"Partner? Like a tennis partner? I'm afraid I don't play."

"I see. I mean partner, as in significant other." She starts clicking her pen while I talk.

"Well, if you read my chart you might learn that I am single. I live alone. When I come home from work I feel relieved that I can be myself. I don't have to pretend to be interested in anything, I don't have to make meaningless conversation, and I don't have to do what other people want me to do." Here I go again. My heart is pounding and my body is tensing up. Tim might be right about my anger.

"So you feel most comfortable when you are alone, and being in situations around others makes you uncomfortable or anxious?" The doctor lifts up her pen and taps it against her temple, almost as if she is signalling that she has grown impatient with my answers.

"Yes." Her tapping has made me feel like nothing more than an object placed in front of her to be solved. She has gathered all her information and is dutifully fulfilling her role as an appointed healer to enlighten me with the solution to my problem. I wonder if she is tapping her pen on purpose to annoy me. After all, that's why I do it.

"I'm going to prescribe you something that will help with your anxiety."

I interrupt the doctor with a sarcastic question, "Will it cure me?"

The doctor breaks character for the first time and shows a sign of emotion by a quiet gasp and retreat in her body language. Apparently robots do have feelings.

"It will help."

"So it won't cure me."

"I am going to prescribe you a medication called Lorazepam. When you start to feel anxious, take one of these pills. It will help mitigate your anxiety. It's not a cure, but I see that you are currently in therapy. You are doing the right thing by seeking help."

"I'm really just here so I can keep my job. I'm kind of addicted to getting a paycheque. You know, I've heard people say money isn't everything, so then why do we need to earn so much of it?" I'm not sure why I'm defensive. Is the doctor on to something? Am I trying to hide a weakness or flaw?

The doctor clicks her pen and slides it back in her breast pocket. She doesn't seem interested in answering my rhetorical question but she also doesn't make any motion to stop me from talking.

"Yes. Money is useful. Be sure to continue with your counselling and follow the prescription. It's an anti-anxiety medication that should help. A pharmacist will be able to explain the side effects and directions for use."

Two hours of waiting and in return I am rewarded with a five-minute diagnosis and a recommendation to dope up. Maybe my problem really is that simple. Maybe that is why I am defensive. I've let myself struggle for so long about something so simple. Damn her for pointing it out.

Chapter 20

I've been walking around a drug store for the past thirty-five minutes trying to work up the resolve to hand my prescription over to a pharmacist. I've been holding a basket in my hand and casually strolling up and down the health and beauty aisles, carefully reading the labels of shampoos and soaps before placing them in my basket.

If I collect my prescription I am admitting I have a problem.

I am surprised to find myself now walking through a grocery section in the drug store. From outside I could tell the drug store is an exceptionally large building, but I wasn't prepared to see that this store is just another giant self-contained shopping centre. When I peer out from the cereal aisle, I can see video games, movies, and electronics. If I retrace my steps back to the aisles containing personal cleansing products, I'll be across from nutritional supplements and exercise equipment. People entering the store are confronted with a maze of books and magazines that leads them directly into fragrances and cosmetics. Have we loosened the definition of drugs to include consumer products? Are people who struggle with an insatiable desire to be consumers actually drug addicts? Exhilarated by the release of adrenaline and endorphins that accompany the experience of a purchase, buying makes us feel temporarily complete. Each new purchase brings us instant gratification and escape from the pain of living. I see no difference between a heroin addict shooting up to find instant gratification and the consumerist junkie buying the latest model of phone or most popular style of jacket to find instant gratification. They must have their buy. Kids will scream and cry until they get their fix and adults will bury themselves in debt just to get their high.

I can see a junkie across from me in the electronics section now. He's holding up a new release close to his face, examining the holographic slip cover and shiny lettering. *Furious 7*, it seems the studios didn't have enough time to include "Fast and The" on the cover this time round. Right in the middle of the cover I can see a large blue sticker that proudly displays its high price and disclaimer about being the extended edition. It seems they charge you more for every bonus Vin Diesel grunt they added back into the film. An additional run time of seven minutes. Only the affluent can afford to garner pleasure from this particular item, and I am not surprised to see the man smile as he puts it in his basket. The man starts to walk in my direction. His sleek leather shoes are accented by the rolled up cuffs of his dark blue jeans. This man could be the cover model for a Banana Republic advertisement – casual but with a visibly expensive flair. Peering into his basket as he walks by I can see Calvin Klein cologne, protein powder, and a collection of skin care products: almond butter scrub, anti-aging cream for under the eyes, paste that promises a look comparable to windblown hair, and shaving cream made from natural, organic ingredients. Car keys hang from the fingers in his free hand, flaunting his BMW key fob to everyone in the store.

The middle class suburban warrior, fighting to keep his jeans designer and car luxury.

Christ, why am I still loitering in the drug store? People come here all the time to get weird prescriptions filled out; I'm sure I'll just be another in a long line of unhealthy people submitting to the recommendation of a doctor. I abandon the cereal aisle and make my way to the front counter of the pharmacy with one hand in my pocket. I clutch the prescription in anticipation of having to pull it out. This isn't the worst thing that could happen to me, and at least there isn't a line up. I put my basket down and rest one hand on the counter. From out of the corner of my eye I can see the male suburban warrior flirting with an attractive woman in the aisle containing braces for muscle injuries and hot/cold pads. She's touching her shoulder and making faces; now he's touching her shoulder and they're both laughing. I can barely pull it together to approach someone who is paid to interact with me, and here is this man casually flirting with an attractive woman in a drug store.

"Can I help you? Sir?"

If I turn away and never look back, it will be as if the man and woman never existed in the first place. Seeing other people happy makes me feel like I've somehow done something wrong with my life.

"I have a prescription." I am now resting both hands on the counter.

The pharmacist leans in closer to me and says, "Do you happen to have it with you?"

"Of course, yes. It's in my pocket. Sorry." This feels eerily similar to buying drugs from that older guy everyone knew in high school. The pharmacist is so cool it makes me nervous. The only thing I can do is try and reciprocate his coolness. Of course, trying to reciprocate someone's natural coolness can only result in making myself look like a total idiot. The pharmacist reviews my prescription and with a smile he politely tells me to wait a moment. He turns around to a girl sitting hunched over on a stool and hands her my prescription. She doesn't seem too enthusiastic about the exchange, but it does seem to make her get up and start fiddling around with the small boxes and containers located behind her. The pharmacist turns back to me,

"Have you ever taken Lorazepam before?"

"No."

"Are you currently on any other kind of medication?"

"No."

"Do you have any allergies?"

"No."

"The medication you've been prescribed, Lorazepam, is an anti-anxiety medication. It works by reducing the activity of nerves in the brain. So when you start to feel worked up, when your anxiety becomes overwhelming to the point that you are having trouble thinking, acting, and concentrating, taking one pill will help calm the overactivity occurring in your brain."

"I see. So thinking too much is my problem."

"Well, an abundance of activity in your brain may be a reason for your anxiety. Do not exceed three pills in one day. Take a pill when you feel like you are experiencing very high amounts of anxiety, it will provide short-term relief from the stress. Do not take with alcohol. You will also benefit from staying hydrated while taking the medication. It may cause dizziness, drowsiness, weakness, headaches, and dry mouth."

"So the solution to my anxiety is to potentially give myself a headache and make myself dizzy, thirsty, physically weak, and tired?"

The pharmacist laughs. "Well, these are potential side effects. You may feel nothing, you may feel one of these symptoms, or you may feel all of them. If the side effects are overwhelming, stop taking the medication immediately and consult a physician. You have been prescribed a short-term dosage, enough for a month. If your treatment is to persist you will need to consult a physician."

"You said it only provides temporary relief from symptoms, so how is it supposed to make me any better?"

"Are you currently in therapy?" The pharmacist is standing tall and upright over me from the counter. The actual pharmacy seems to be raised far above ground level on some sort of pedestal. As if I didn't feel small enough already, I have to be physically lowered before the pharmacist.

"Do you need to know?"

"No. I don't." At this point the hunchback girl drops off a small orange container of pills in front of the pharmacist. He doesn't even thank her, and she just goes right back to her stool to sit hunched over.

"No, I don't need to know. Lorazepam will help provide short-term relief, but if you aren't already, you should consider therapy. There are group therapy sessions that can assist with anxiety. That is a good place to start."

A drug dealer recommending I don't become reliant on his product – the world is full of small surprises.

Chapter 21

My erratic behaviour at work has sparked a rather intrusive response. I am required to attend counselling sessions, I am not to go into work for two weeks, and I am to start taking prescribed medication immediately. Apparently two weeks is all a person needs to be cured of unsightly behavioural issues.

I've spent an entire day in my apartment with little to do but think. I haven't made my mind up about taking the pills. My initial reaction was an unwavering resolve to not swallow one dammed pill. Although, after a single day of solitude, boredom has piqued my interest.

Maybe happiness is just a pill away.

I slowly sit up on the couch where I have been lying for the better part of the day. The day somehow turned to night while I was bedridden with lethargy. I can feel the tension in my lower back and stiffness in my neck as my body becomes flush with blood from muscle activity. I'm fairly confident I'm too stiff to turn my head to the left or right, and I doubt my lower back will let me rotate my body in any direction, but it doesn't matter. I'm holding the bottle of pills right in front of me. My grip slowly becomes tighter. Closing my eyes I seriously consider taking my medication. I consider doing what I'm told.

"Take the pill," I mumble quietly to myself. The silence of the room starts to pound in my head. Each pulse of blood sent from my heart through all of my extremities is echoing through my eardrums. Thump. Thump. Thump. Thump. Thump. The constant static hum of the room has drowned out any noise from the street and the apartments around me.

"Take the pill," I tell myself in a stern voice. "Take the pill."

"Take ... the ... pill..."

"TAKE THE PILL."

Overcome with erratic rage, saliva is dripping from my mouth and my fist is clenched as hard as I can make it. I open my eyes and can see that my hand has gone pale and is shaking slightly. My heart is racing, my teeth are clenched, and I've got a noticeable high from the adrenaline. I slowly bring my free hand up to the lid of the bottle, but as I finger the ridges of the cap, my brain signals me to throw the bottle as far away from me as I can. I am merely a puppet for my brain, so I do as the chemical messages instruct and hurl the bottle into the corner of the living room. It takes a few loud bounces that echo throughout my apartment before it rolls into a dead stop under my bookshelf. I've cast darkness onto my happiness.

Maybe it's about time I got off the couch.

I stand up and start to pace around the living room, walking laps around my coffee table. If I have a problem, and the pill is my solution, then why has no one made an effort to identify what caused the problem in the first place? I am put into treatment and provided medication all too routinely, as if it was expected that I would seek anti-depressants and counselling. Neither the doctor nor the forms I filled out seemed to be concerned with what might have precipitated my bout of mental instability. Our entire practice of health care is predicated on after the fact treatment. A staggering amount of deaths that could have been prevented through lifestyle changes and preventative knowledge occur every year. As a society we don't educate, motivate, or make it a priority to help people make the necessary lifestyle choices to improve physical, emotional, and social health. On the contrary, the American lifestyle seems to ensure that your health will be out of balance by making unhealthy food cheap and unavoidable, keeping wages low and debts high, ensuring long hours are spent at work while little time is spent in the pursuit of leisure or fitness, and constantly raising the price of gym memberships. The sick are big business in America, and the majority of people are uninsured or underinsured and face hefty medical bills for preventable conditions caused by stress, diet, and lack of exercise. It's incredible that no one questions a system that pushes people into illness so that they can charge exorbitant amounts of money for treatment. Of course, the rising costs of eating well, exercising, and finding peace of mind may eventually result in the wholesale adoption of preventative care as a cultural mindset – but not until there is enough profit to be made from it. In a world enamoured with the accumulation of wealth, the health and wellbeing of the general population is not a priority unless it becomes a profitable business venture.

Why am I unable to just take my pill and shut up? Where does all this anger and self-righteousness come from?

Chapter 22

Tim winces slightly before asking me what bothered me so much about the commercial I saw last night.

"It was a beer commercial that starts out with smiling, happy people on a beach. It suddenly cuts to a different set of people on a boat, then people walking on a boardwalk. Some voice smugly asks me if I have laughed enough, had enough fun, made enough memories. It tells me to live life to the fullest, then ends by flashing a box of their beer on screen. What the hell does any of that have to do with beer? If I drink their beer, am I living life to the fullest? If I drink enough, well maybe then I could feign contentment. You can't really live life to the fullest when you have to get up for work every Monday."

"It doesn't sound like you're annoyed with the commercial as much as you feel frustrated that work is keeping you from enjoying life, is that it? You're frustrated and disillusioned."

It's not often anyone is able to say anything that really means anything to me. Tim has managed to knock the wind out of me with a single sentence. As soon as I regain my composure, I know I have to respond, but in a way that provides no further insight into my psyche. No doubt Tim can read my face as well as the sudden shift in my body language.

"Doesn't work distract us all from what life could be? We spend our childhood in school under pressure to decide what job we want to do for the rest of our lives. We're prodded, tested, and forced into jobs based on our performance. When we're young, we're told we can be anything we want to be. As we grow up, we learn that's not true. We really can't be anything we want to be. We can only be what our test scores say we can be. You know what my test scores said I could be? They said I could be unremarkable. They said I will work a frivolous job that does nothing to better society, that does nothing to better myself. Imagination, freedom, and sense of purpose will not be required, so I might as well forget about those. Obedience, acceptance, and apathy about my future, that is what my tests recommended me."

"Your tests recommended it, or you settled for it? Is settling why you feel so frustrated?"

"Isn't that the point, Tim? We can't all be Bill Gates, so we are conditioned into settling for mediocrity. Societies have always found a way to crush the spirit of its lowest members. Why do you think people spend so much time worshipping celebrities? Any chance to live vicariously through someone whose life stands out."

"That's one way of looking at life, but you're going to struggle to find much joy if you think the world is conspiring against you. I can assure you, it's not."

"You can assure me."

"Yes." Tim comes across as bored. I can see it in his eyes, they're freshly glazed in indifference. "You know, you seem to evade conversation about your feelings. Have you noticed this?"

"I can't say that I have."

"I see. Well, I'd still like you to think about how you *feel*. Start to shift your focus away from thoughts and intellectualizing your problems, and towards mindful feeling. Is that something you might be willing to try with me?"

"Are these not feelings?" I cross my arms unsure how I've been scant with feelings.

"No. They are arguments, hypothesis, and all sorts of conjecture. No feeling though." Life suddenly sparks in Tim's eyes. "A feeling is short. Anger. Sadness. Despair. Do you see what I mean? Would you be willing to work on expressing your feelings and moving away from ideas and theories?"

"Well, what good will that do? Are my ideas not what I am struggling with?"

Tim nods his head. "It may seem like the origin of your struggles. However, they are just the leaves of a tree. The root is where your feelings are. If you're feeling sad, disappointed when you're at work – that is the root. You could get another job and still feel sad and disappointed because you never really dove into why you feel that way."

A new debate, how titillating. "But if I were to resolve everything I've said before, would that not solve my problem?"

I put Tim in check, but it may be premature to declare a checkmate. Tim seems confident in how he will handle my response. "You are referring to the whole society piece, wages, school, all of that." Boredom seeps back into Tim's eyes and finds its way into his breath. "Is that something you can really solve? If it changed, you had a better wage, and more opportunity, would you suddenly feel better? Would you be happy?"

"I'm … not sure" Leaning back into my chair, I start to see Tim's point. Am I just making up excuses to rationalize how I feel, displace blame onto anything but myself?

"I'd also like you to consider this: what good does blaming the world for your problems do? Do you have any sort of agency? Your feelings though, those are your responsibility. You own those, no one else does. If we just accept that to be true, for the sake of argument, what difference might that make in your outlook?"

"Well. Hypothetically, if I were to accept that as true." Clasping my hands together I start rubbing my thumb against my palm. "I suppose that would mean, if I were feeling unhappy, that it would be my fault. Not school, or work."

"Right." Tim smiles. "And if it was your fault, then that would mean you are also the source of the solution. Would you agree?"

Shrinking into my chair I cooperatively mutter, "Yes."

"Good. I think we've made some progress. I don't want to keep pushing this point, the idea of blame and responsibility. I hope it is ok if I change the topic for now, I'm sure we will find more opportunity to explore them." Tim smiles and releases a deep breath. "Have you been taking your pills?"

"You've already asked me that, Tim."

"I suppose I did." Tim shifts his weight and eyes me carefully. "You never really answered me. Have you been taking your pills?"

"No. I have not been. I thought about it, I really did." It's difficult to understand why we tell the truth when pressured. All it takes is someone to look you in your eye, and not just a surface glance. If you really look into someone's eyes and connect with them, it has a special way of inducing panic. Lying becomes almost impossible

"Hm. So you thought about it and didn't see a reason to take one."

"Correct."

"Tell me then, how do you ..."

"Feel about taking the pills?"

Tim smiles. "Becoming predictable, am I? It's a fair question. You've thought a lot. Rationalized a lot. But what is going on inside?"

I sigh and rub my eyes. "I suppose I feel ... like I don't want to take a pill."

Tim is nodding his head, planning his next move. "You haven't felt a need to take it. You're not feeling anxious or uncomfortable."

"Well, I wouldn't say that."

"What would you say?" Tim leans forward in his chair. I believe he is trying to indicate his interest in my response through his body language.

I'm finding it hard to make eye contact. I'm not really sure how to respond to Tim. "I guess I never really saw myself as someone needing medication. Maybe part of me doesn't want to admit there is anything wrong."

"That's interesting. So you think there may be something wrong?"

Nodding my head I try desperately to find a window in Tim's office to look out of. Anything to escape this conversation. I look back over at Tim who is waiting for a response, and wonder what does he expect from me right now? A big, emotional disclosure, replete with tears and sad stories about my childhood? How is talking supposed to change anything for me?

"I'll admit, it seems like there may be something ... not right. Not sure I can put it into words."

"That must be difficult for you. You're very articulate, yet you can't find words to describe what you are experiencing."

Silence.

"Do you mind if we try something before our next session? I'd like you to consider writing down your thoughts *and* feelings next time you are considering taking your pill. Whether you do or don't take your pill, I want you to try writing. See if this process helps you articulate what is happening, especially what you are feeling inside. Is that something you are willing to try?"

"I suppose I could give it a shot." I've got a sour taste in my mouth. I really don't want to humour Tim and spend time writing down my thoughts and feelings.

Am I able to admit what I feel?

Chapter 23

Fashion. An idea invented by humans. What is considered an acceptable fashion trend drastically changes every five years so that we have a reason to single out people who fail to blend in. Nothing builds confidence like the false sense of superiority afforded by popularity. Wearing the latest trend allows us to superficially exclude those who can't afford or don't understand that clothes help define where we fit in the strata of social hierarchy. People who reside at the top are rewarded with the unquestioned power to insult and humiliate those who choose to wallow at the bottom of the trendy social ladder. Charles Darwin would most likely approve of how society has chosen to structure itself. Those empowered by a sense of entitlement resulting from their resoundingly fashionable choice of attire beat out those with a weak sense of fashion. Despite their claims, men and women do pursue partners higher in the evolutionary chain of fashion because they show an insatiable desire to thrive and adapt to their trendy environment, and will thereby likely provide the trendiest offspring with the greatest chance of popularity in high school.

I am watching these trendy fucks in a Starbucks. If I were to turn on a television or open one of those pop-culture magazines that are unburdened by any semblance of valuable content, I would see images of everyone in this room. What is it with trends? Some asshole on TV ties a plaid shirt around his waist and suddenly everyone mimics the action. People desperate to fit in instantly adopt any clothing, phrase, or mannerism that they see on television. The biggest irony is how people are convinced that buying into a fashion trend can help them become unique and special. Dressing up to look unique or special only results in being even more like everyone else.

I see four haircuts that match Scarlett Johansson's from the cover of *Cosmo*. I spy with my little eye several men who are sporting the same hairstyle as Ryan Gosling. Too bad it's not Scarlett's and Ryan's haircuts that men and women pine after. Their conversations appear to be as ephemeral as their choice in clothing. The most substantive conversation I can discern appears to be about whether Michelle, the main character of a reality dating show, should choose Dan or Kyle, contestants on the show. The conversation appears to be heated as they can't agree on who the most eligible bachelor for Michelle is. Nothing worth hearing, and nothing worth saying. These people have come so far in life only to say so little to each other. Subject matter has hit an all time low in the fluctuating peaks and valleys of public discourse.

What do I have to add to the pool of meaningful conversation? Do I really have anything better to say than what I'm hearing around me? The fact I'm sitting alone likely speaks volumes to one of these truths; maybe I should open myself up to the possibility that it is the less flattering of the two truths.

Sitting in Starbucks was a mistake. I came here to regain focus after my recent session with Tim, but all I can focus on is how stupid the guy at the front counter ordering his latte looks. He has one of those hats that sags further down the back of his head than his eyeline. His shirt is so tight and short that it's impossible not to notice the underwear band peeking from the top of his low hanging, skin tight pants. It's hard to imagine why this man chooses to wear skin tight pants, and then consciously pulls them down below his hip bone so that an unavoidable sag in the butt of his pants appears. His pants look like an adult diaper with long legs. The trendsetting man who appears to be around twenty-five or twenty-six years old is now joining a group of similarly garbed trendsetters. They all appear to be twenty-five or twenty-six, but are dressed like teenagers in long legged, adult diapers. Judging by their conversation, they must be recent university graduates. They are in an intense discussion about which Bon Iver album is better.

Best album. Best in what way? It inspires the greatest recall of fond memories? The music moves you to tears? Maybe if I take these pills I will be able to drone on about what the best flavour of M and M's is in public. The vapid ambience of Starbucks has derailed my attempt at introspection. Perhaps cafés are no longer the hub of intellectual expansion. Some of the first cafés originated in Persia and were used to discuss politics, recite poetry, and play chess. Currently, in the United States of America, cafés provide a comfortable setting for small talk and gossip. Casually putting my hand into my pocket I fish out the small orange pill container and hold it tightly in my left hand. OK. It's in my hands. Now what. I've reached the crossroads where Tim suggested I write down thoughts and feelings about the pill that surface. I didn't bring anything to write on, so this napkin under my drink will have to serve as a makeshift journal for today. My thoughts … what am I thinking? With my right hand I pull a pen out of my pocket and draw it close to the napkin. Thoughts. Closing my eyes and squeezing my left hand tightly over the pill container, I consider what I should write down.

Opening my eyes I make my first stab at the napkin.

I've always had an aversion to taking medication. Good start. *I feel pressured.* Maybe Tim will get off my case now that I've expressed a feeling.

Why do I feel pressured? Who is pressuring? Pushing my pen into the napkin I see the ink starting to bleed into the fibres.

I want control. I don't want to give away control. Is it control to abstain from treatment, or is that giving up control?

On a roll I consider my next thought. What prompted me to even pull out the pill container? Sitting in Starbucks, listening to all the garbage unfolding around me. It's clear. *I don't like being around others. I feel angry. Frustrated. Disconnected. Everyone flows in the same direction while I fight against the current.*

I am always on guard.

I put my thumb on the small triangle located on the lid of the pill container and gently push until it pops off. With little concern over who's watching I shake out one of the round tablets and choke it back with an overpriced Starbucks coffee.

Four billion prescriptions were written for drugs by doctors in America last year. I suppose it was only a matter of time before it was my turn to get with the program.

I am still in control. My guard remains vigilant.

Chapter 24

I don't know what I expected, but as I plod though the ever-flowing river of people on the sidewalk I notice no discernible change in the way I feel. I assumed taking medication would provide me with a euphoric calm, allowing me to brush off the typical angst I feel about strangers shouldering me on the street.

People look right through me.

The longer I walk, the more I start to feel something new. My mind is normally burdened with perpetual dialogue, constantly overanalyzing the glare I receive from a passerby that I smile at, or the oversaturation of advertisements along the downtown walkway. But currently my footsteps are being met with silence. Every thump of my heels as my feet hit the pavement has replaced all thought. This is the closest I have ever felt to being a robot. I am engaging in bipedal motion as if automated to perform the task. Had my mind been able to process a thought I might have finally come to understand why no one ever moves out of my way on the street. I might also have noticed that I just walked into O'Flaherty's and am now standing tall and stoic in the inside entrance.

"Haven't seen your ugly mug in a while," Jeff nudges me from the side in a playful fashion.

I give Jeff a friendly slap on the shoulder, and respond, "No kidding. I've been off work."

"Do you mind getting the fuck out of the doorway?" Some uptight lady in a drab sweater has her hands placed firmly on her hips. Apparently I am in her way, and she's never heard of politely asking a stranger to accommodate her needs.

"Relax, he's coming in." Jeff gives the lady his back and pulls me towards the bar. "Why don't you grab a seat with us? You aren't here with anyone, are you?"

"No, no. I just ... I was in the neighbourhood, and sort of just stopped in. I guess I just had a sudden impulse."

"Yah yah, you just knew we're always here Fridays after work and you just missed us, admit it."

"Friday, it's Friday?" I scratch my head. The days of the week don't seem to hold as much significance when you're not required to be at work. No need to celebrate the absence of work when every day is a Saturday.

"Hey Steve, Mary, look what just walked in." Jeff strolls up to the side table just to the left of the bar that Steve and Mary are seated at. Casually motioning his thumb in a pointing motion, he takes his seat.

"Well, grab a seat, stranger. We'll get you a glass." Steve leans back and catches the eye of the bartender.

"Steve, Mary, how are you?" I find myself smiling as I take my seat. I don't think I've ever asked my coworkers how they felt before.

"Wow, time off must be helping. I don't think you've ever asked me how I am before." Mary confirms my previous absence of affective inquiries.

"It seemed like the thing to say. I've been watching a lot of television, picked up some new social cues." The table simultaneously erupts into laughter. Apparently not only am I more concerned about the feelings of my colleagues, but now I am lightening the mood with a newfound sense of humour.

The pill must be taking effect. I am not myself. My hand is casually resting on the back of Mary's chair. I am engaging and humorous. My mind is as blank as it was when I walked into the pub. I am on autopilot. What's even stranger is Mary, Steve, and Jeff don't seem to be thrown off by my alien behaviour.

I've felt this way before.

"Excuse me, I have to use the bathroom." I manage to regain control of my thoughts and body and make a hasty retreat to the washroom. I'm trying to recall the past few times I was at the pub, but the strain on my mind is immense. It's as if I am fighting to be heard in my own mind, but fighting what?

I've felt this way before.

I remember now. Every time I was at this pub, I drank myself stupid. Every drink I had, I lost just a little bit of control over myself. Every drink I had made me feel like someone else, until I was someone else. Mary's comments the other week make sense now. She thought I was acting cold, but I was just acting sober. I was acting like the bitter, jaded person I am.

Maybe happiness really is just a pill away.

Looking up from the sink I gather what little resolve I have. My mind is struggling to hold control, to force me to leave and go home. I don't want to be here, I hate these people and this place … but I'm too quiet. Without thinking, I pull the container of pills from my pocket and swiftly pull one out and slip it into my mouth. I don't even take a drink of water from the tap, I just swallow it spitefully. I catch a spiteful glare from my reflection in the mirror. My self-concept has been so tied into the way I was … the way I am. If I change, will I still be me?

Chapter 25

"So what were you meant for?"

"...Pardon?"

"What were you meant for? You just mentioned you don't feel like you were meant for working nine to five every day. So what did you dream about doing when you grew up, what do you feel you were meant for?"

Tim's office. The rich aroma of my leather chair reminds me how rare it is to sit on the real deal. My feet share in the experience as they rest on the leather ottoman carefully positioned to support my legs and spine. All of Tim's furniture is ergonomically designed to promote proper posture and relaxation, which seems paradoxical because I am usually most comfortable when I'm slouching. I'm trying to focus on his question: "What were you meant for?" Seems like a veiled attempt at uncovering what job will cause me the least amount of anxiety.

"We aren't meant for anything. There is no grand plan for anyone. Fate does not influence or determine any outcomes in our lives. No omnipotent deity has decided our actions, and nothing was meant to be. It simply happens. We all make choices, and our choices dictate what unfolds. I never tried hard enough in math class, so I guess I screwed myself from ever working for NASA."

"So you don't feel like anyone was just meant to be something."

"Context often provides a helping hand. If you're the son or daughter of a movie star, you're likely to be a movie star. It's not fate, magic, or destined to be … some people just happen to have the right parents. Look, if I go outside and happen to catch a taxi, it's because I happen to exist in the same time and space as a vacant taxi. The world didn't will me into it. It just happens." The hostility in my voice is apparent, even to me.

What were you meant for? This question has always drawn ire from me. It relies far too heavily on the ill-conceived concept of destiny. It's like telling someone they are meant to eat a salad three years from now on a Tuesday evening. It's presumptuous to assume you can predict the future with any kind of certainty, let alone make the case that some higher power mapped out the events of your life. People are drawn to two things: what is comfortable and what is interesting. If someone follows their interest with enough determination and drive, they will likely reach some semblance of their original goal. If a kid grows up and becomes an astronaut, his parents will tell everyone it was fate. It was fate because their kid always dreamed about reaching the stars and he idolized Neil Armstrong and Buzz Aldrin. Let's ignore how hard this child had to work in math and science. Let's ignore how hard it was as an adult to always rise to the top of every class, to stand out both physically and intellectually. The personal sacrifices this spaceman made are overlooked and ignored because fate is a more romantic thought than years of hard work. Of course, hard work only gets you as far as context and happenstance allow. For every person that became an astronaut, there were likely a hundred dreamers forced to pivot from their goal of going to space. The story of failure and moving on may be the most important lesson to share, yet those tales are buried in the wake of linear success stories.

The majority of us choose to walk the path of least resistance. We allow ourselves to fall into whatever will get us somewhere that is socially acceptable and results in the least amount of criticism from the people that we know. When other people attain success, we immediately ignore the amount of effort the person exerted because it intimidates us. Likely, we are just trying to insulate ourselves from the possibility of failure. After all, success is a combination of effort, ability, and happenstance. If we can't stomach effort without hitting the outcome we set in our sights, what then?

I am walking the path of least resistance.

Tim allows a minute to pass. We both feel the air of hostility that has filled the room.

"The outcome of your life seems to upset you. That is a theme that has come up often. You're not happy with how your life has turned out."

"No. I guess I'm not. If I was happy about how life turned out, I don't suppose I'd be in your chair now, would I, Tim."

"Mmm." Tim just nods and leans forward. "You know, I don't think many people are happy with the way their lives turned out. It's part of growing up, part of being an adult."

"Isn't that sad? Doesn't it get you that everyone has just accepted how shitty life is? So many people just accept that they have to be poor or work a job they don't like to get by. I can't seem to reconcile that. I can't reconcile that this is all I'll ever be, some guy working his ass off every Monday to Friday until I'm old enough to retire. I'm waiting for life to pass me by so I can retire and enjoy having free time when I'm too old to do anything with it."

"That's a pretty profound realization to make. You're stuck on how awful everything is, and miss how great some things can be."

"How great things can be. Do you buy lottery tickets?"

"Well, I'm not sure how that's relevant." Tim leans back into his chair, seemingly taken aback by my question.

"Please, just indulge me, Tim. Do you buy lottery tickets?"

"Well, yes. Like many people I buy a lottery ticket every once in a while."

"You ever think about why you buy lottery tickets, why anyone does? It's not just a chance to win money. It's a chance out of life. It's the golden ticket to freedom. It's still the eleven-hundreds, and we're still just serfs tied to the land, toiling away under the purview of our lord of the manor, just waiting to die. Winning the lottery is your ticket out of a life of servitude."

"I suppose that's a way to look at it. Maybe I just buy lottery tickets for the sake of buying them."

"Maybe. But somehow I doubt it." Another long drawn out pause – maybe I've hit a nerve with Tim. He's supposed to be counselling me, and yet I always end up in an existential debate about life. Maybe if I keep at it, Tim will stop sleeping his way through life and be just as pissed off about everything as I am.

"Well. Looks like we are reaching the end of another session. I'm curious if you've tried that activity we talked about and written down your thoughts and feelings."

"Surprisingly, I did."

"Hmm." Tim purrs at my response yet again. "I'm curious why you chose to say 'surprisingly'."

It feels like several minutes pass before I find the words to assemble an answer. "At first, I didn't want to do it. Maybe just because you told me to."

"You feel I forced you into doing it."

"I suppose you never really said that I *had* to do it, but I walked away with that feeling." I take a deep breath in and exhale what feels like defeat.

"You didn't want to do it. But you did." Tim is squinting his eyes at me now. It looks like he is thinking through my motivations.

"That's right. I even used a napkin."

"I get the sense that your following through on the activity isn't the only part that surprised you."

"That's right." I sound interested in Tim's insight. So this is what it's like to have an engaging conversation. "What really surprised me was how I kept going. Compelled to continue, almost."

"Did you arrive at any interesting insight?"

"I like to be in control."

"Hmm." Tim nods his head several times before smiling. "I've often felt that when we talk. It comes across in the way you communicate."

It's my turn to purr this time. "Hmm."

"I wonder," Tim pauses to lean forward and stroke his chin, "if you could expand on that thought. You like to be in control. What does control look like for you?"

"It's difficult to say."

Tim looks disappointed, yet maintains interest in the tone of his voice. "Often when we speak, it feels like you are holding on tight to control your emotions. I find myself wondering if you do this to control how I may perceive you. To influence what I think about you, and maybe even how you perceive yourself."

I want to be mad at Tim right now. Not for any slight, rather for holding up a mirror to my ugliness.

"I also wrote that I always feel on guard."

"It's interesting you would say that, just now." Tim uses his hands to accent the word 'now' by pointing at the ground.

"Is it?" I'm not really sure what to say anymore. I'm really not in control anymore.

"I shared my perception of you. It wasn't entirely flattering." Pause for effect. "You responded by telling me you feel you are guarded. I certainly felt another wall come up between us there. Do you feel the wall as well?"

"I think I do. It can't be very high though … you keep climbing over it." Was that another brick in the wall?

"I'm starting to feel progress in you. I hope you feel it as well. What you've told me, that you like to be in control and feel like you are always on guard, describes the barrier I feel between us when we talk. This wall you put up between you and others, what does it give you?"

Tim's comfort with silence is remarkable. He lets me marinate in his question until I'm tender enough to respond. "I suppose I feel comfortable behind a wall. Safe."

"Comfortable. Safe."

Like a reflex, I flail into a response without thinking. "That's exactly how I feel. Like I can actually relax."

"You can't relax around others?"

"When I put up a wall, I can." I make sense, right?

"So you are constantly building walls between you and others to feel relaxed. That sounds exhausting. Like the work never ends." I have never experienced someone being so polite about telling me how wrong I am.

"… Yes … it is." I can't lay brick fast enough to keep pace with Tim. He's right, I'm lying to myself if I think putting up a barrier actually relaxes me. My work never ends.

Crossing his legs, Tim changes the direction of the conversation. "What does building a wall take away from you?"

"Closeness. Any chance of you getting near me."

"Wow." Tim uncrosses his legs and leans towards me again. "That is a powerful statement. It seems like all your brick work keeps you too busy to get near me as well. Likely this is the case with others in your life." Glancing at the clock, Tim shifts gears again. "I'm conscious of our time together and I don't want to push too far and abruptly stop. I think we have some interesting thoughts to talk about next meeting. I'd like to explore more about these walls you build."

"Maybe I'll write about that." Smiling, I'm glad we are drawing to a close.

"There is one last question I need to ask. Have you been taking your medication?"

Tim has a gentle way of knocking down barriers to get where he needs to go.

"...Yes."

"Good. Have you felt any different? Have you noticed any positive results?"

"They uh, they've quieted my mind. I don't think as much when I take them."

"That's good to hear. It must be nice to relax your mind a little. Well, keep following through with your prescription. I also know of some group counselling sessions you might find helpful."

Why is he talking so much? I thought we had reached the end of the session. I just want to leave but he keeps going on, and on.

"...people working through similar problems and..."

I'm clenching my jaw and nodding my head. I'm not sure how much longer I can sit here exposed.

"...people working through issues just like you. I've seen a lot of positive results from people who have attended..."

Tim's pep talk has effectively pulled me from the conversation.

"You're progressing very well. You have some anxiety towards work and your control in life, I think together we can help you learn to manage better. Maybe even grow." Tim slinks back into his chair and folds his hands. Smiling politely, I can hear the cry of smug air bellowing from his nostrils and revealing his innermost thoughts.

I've done a good job. Look at me. I know what's best for everyone. I am the gate-keeper of sanity.

"I think you're almost ready to resume work. We'll meet again in a few days."

Resume work. That's *exactly* what I wanted to hear. *Oh, since you've been away from work you've suddenly started to get better. Let's send you back to work; you don't have enough stress.*

There is no reprieve from responsibility.

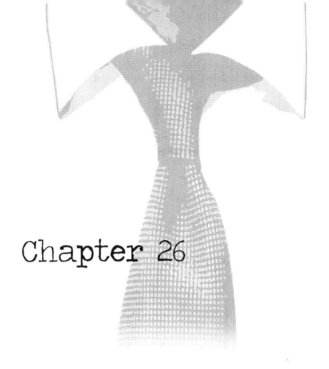

Chapter 26

Decades ago science fiction authors painted a picture of our present where we drove hover cars, colonized planets, and integrated artificial intelligence into our technology. Here we sit, still driving cars with wheels, confined to our own planet, and without the use of artificial intelligence. Somewhere along the way human development seems to have reached a plateau. We landed on the moon in the 1960s using slide rules and tin foil. But in an age where computers can process a million mathematical equations simultaneously, we've failed to advance to the level romanticized for us. The underlying problem is not that the human race lacks the potential to advance any further; rather, the problem is that the human race currently lacks the overall intelligence to reach a higher plane of existence. A computer processes millions of mathematical equations simultaneously. Yet, the average human is unable to multiply two single digit numbers without the aid of calculator. Just as a herd of buffalo can only travel as fast as its slowest member, the human race, too, can only advance as far as its dumbest members. In order for the future that was so often fantasized about to become reality, today's genius must become tomorrow's dolt. The Carl Sagans, Neil deGrasse Tysons, and Noam Chomskys of the world must become the bar for average or less than average. As long as the basics behind math, philosophy, history, and science elude common man, how can we expect the human race to leave our own terrestrial borders? That is one thing Star Trek got right. You can't find a single character on that show who doesn't have a high level understanding of physics, science, math, philosophy, history and engineering. Star Trek is the story of geniuses gallivanting around the galaxy, only they don't consider themselves anything but the norm. Even hyper aggressive Klingons have a mastery of science, math, and engineering.

Intelligence has never really thrived in the mainstream and often results in the spurning of overachievers from the general population. The fact that we label individuals who are motivated to learn as overachievers is emblematic of our self-destructive desire to remain in the cave. Desirable limits of intellectual attainment are maintained through emotional and physical abuse. Bullies are the police force of the dull-witted, ensuring that the pursuit of knowledge is swiftly punished. Popular people have managed to systematically halt the advancement of society to avoid expending the effort necessary to increase their brain function. Attractive individuals with charm, charisma, and natural athletic ability don't have to rely on intelligence or critical thought. They don't need to understand the purpose of higher order thinking because they won't face a situation where their physical appearance, charm, or physical prowess isn't enough to get them through. Everything in life has come so easily to these attractive people that the thought of hard work, sacrifice, and the failure required to learn and grow is terrifying. The result has been the intentional dumbing down of society so that the pretty people can spare themselves the hardship of cultivating their minds. But as I finish my thought, I think about what Tim said about my anger and discontentment from how my life has turned out. For the first time, I start to feel awful about the way I think and how I quick I am to lay blame. My anger has become a filter for how I perceive life. All I do is think in broad generalizations that do nothing but feed my emotion. Emotion that I've been denying because I don't understand. How do I feel Tim? I feel angry and all my thoughts feed my anger. I don't even know what the hell I am angry about.

I am sitting behind the wheel of my car alone and overwhelmed by the desire to stay in my car. I want silence and reprieve from the mirror that's been following me around lately. I turn the key and silence the engine and the final clicks and exasperated gasps of the engine whimper into silence as it cools down.

I am in the parking lot of a community recreation centre. This is the location of a group that Tim recommended. It's not often I take the advice of others or willingly place myself in a social situation, but I guess I've been questioning myself a lot lately. It's almost as if I watched myself drive here, and now I'm just trying to find the self-control to turn my car back on and get the hell out of here.

No such luck. Like a sheep following the herd, I instinctively get out of my car and join the small group of people shuffling through the parking lot towards the entrance of the community centre. Entering the building, I am immediately halted by a geriatric pylon inside the foyer. With his slacks pulled up high and tied tight across his waste by a wicker belt, the old man blocks the straight path and signals us to walk to the left with a wave of his hand. There's not much expression on his face or life in his eyes. He is a machine programmed to shepherd visitors … a terminator sent back in time to kill our option to walk straight after entering the building. I am now part of a herd of unwanted and dishevelled human beings, mindlessly walking the only path provided. The hallway is decorated with carefully spaced posters directing us to the room holding our group counselling session. This is odd, since there is only one room in this hallway and it is located at the very end of the path. There is literally no way we could get lost or wander into the wrong room, yet someone dedicated time and resources to ensure a reminder of where to go was placed every few steps.

The herd reaches the end of the hallway and spills out into a large, plain room. Other than a circle made out of chairs, the room is void of anything. The room is as empty as the souls of its occupants. I can hear the echo from every step I take reverberating off the bare walls. This group is likely the only place any of these people feel special, heard, or normal, which is the source of its allure. I am starting to think wanting to feel normal is what's pulling me in. Why I've been following the crowd dutifully and silently.

"Welcome back, everyone…" The group therapist motions for everyone to take their seats. All conversation stops as we obediently follow directions and take our seats. Some awkward coughs and squeaks from chairs shuffling into position fill the room.

As soon as the room settles, the woman running the group asks us to take turns sharing how we feel. The members just keep going on and on about their feelings. They listen intently to what others have to say. Every comment, gesture, or sudden pause elicits such a strong emotional reaction. The girl to my left is in tears and nodding her head as if she is saying, "yes, yes, YES," to the man pouring out his soul. "Yes! Keep telling us how miserable you are! Yes, please make me cry! Make me feel like I'm not the only loser!"

I feel no desire to cry or to reciprocate any of the emotion displayed by the excessively underweight girl across from me.

Your sad story does nothing for me. I am on guard and in control.

"Wow, this is just some really powerful stuff. It's amazing that we came into this room as strangers, but you are such kind and amazing people that just after a short period we are able to share such intimate details about our lives." The leader of the group is leaning forward in her chair, eyeing every member of the group as if she were assessing the authenticity of their vulnerability.

"It's just such a relief knowing that I'm not alone," says the only other man in the group. All the women around us are nodding their heads, looking around at the other members just to confirm they are nodding their heads too. Even a circle of crazy people has a sophisticated set of social norms that must be followed, and nodding your head in affirmation of everyone's feelings is one of those norms. I've alienated myself from yet another group.

"It's just so touching to hear..."

I

"...these wonderful comments that..."

just

"...people I just met today..."

can't

"...I've been such a wreck the past few weeks..."

relate

"...and I just feel like, well I am just happy that..."

to

"...It's such a relief to finally have someone listen without..."

you.

"...judging me for the way I feel."

Arms crossed and sitting impassively in my chair I pass on the invitation to share with a gentle shake of my head, prompting the group counsellor to transition us to her next planned activity. She smiles and walks calmly to her stereo, and then with the click of a button I'm bombarded with the sound of the ocean. Or a beach. Not quite sure what the difference in sound would be … either way I hear waves crashing.

"Loneliness is an empty feeling. An unhappy feeling that we get when we feel unwanted." Her pacing is perfect. Every word comes out fully enunciated and projected in a soothing tone.

"Even in the presence of others, we can sometimes still feel lonely. We all have the need to be wanted, to be cared about. Loneliness can feel overwhelming and we may want to try and ignore it. But we can't. We have to look our loneliness in the face and confront it."

I am stuck between two thoughts. Part of me doesn't want to feel, doesn't want to reach out emotionally. It wants to push itself into a comfortable asylum somewhere quiet. Another part of me is desperate for some emotional or physical connection with someone else. A small part of me doesn't want to be alone. I am stuck in between the two thoughts, trapped in inaction. My thoughts seem to tip more and more to the part of me that wants to stay within myself. But these pills … have started to tip the balance of scales. I can hear my negative thoughts about everyone in this room. I am aware of all my justifications to push others away and keep to myself. I can't help but voice in my mind how everyone in this room is so uninteresting. They don't know how to act without leeching off the mannerisms of someone else. I feel turned off. Yet, I also sense jealousy. Jealousy of how others around me have an ability to be part of the world. Maybe I'm the one who doesn't know how to act around others.

Is that what I'm so mad about?

She is talking about loneliness, but how can you really know who you are unless you spend time alone? Protected by the noise of the crowd, we continually avoid meeting ourselves. Each person in this group session is distraught about learning who they are in the absence of other people. I am distraught about other people learning who I am when I'm around others. Unhappy, bitter, and confused. What if I'm wrong? What if we can only understand ourselves in relation to others? How else can I describe myself if I am not comparing myself?

"We are going to face our loneliness today, together. I want you to feel relaxed. Choose a comfortable position, and slowly close your eyes…" Her voice slows to a mesmerizing halt. I almost feel like I have no choice other than to close my eyes. I am under her spell …

"Focus on your breathing. Inhale and exhale normally, but focus on each breath as it comes in, and each breath as it leaves your body."

I never have to meet myself if I stay far enough away from others.

"Like waves washing on the shore, allow each breath to roll in and out. Your breaths are becoming a rhythm, rolling in and rolling out. Rolling in and rolling out. Just like waves rolling into the beach, then slowly retreating. Rolling in, and rolling out. Breathing in, and breathing out."

I am a wave, washing onto the shore. Reaching out to something but being pulled back to where I came from.

"Silently, in your minds, I want you to clear all thoughts by counting. Focus on nothing but the numbers. As we count up from one to five, then back down to one, every breath is a new count."

"One…"

"Two…"

"Three…"

When was the last time I had real contact with another person?

"Four…"

"Five…"

I have no answer.

"Four…"

"Three…"

I can't recall the last real conversation I had with anyone who wasn't my counsellor.

"Two…"

"One…"

"Two…"

"Three…"

"Four…"

Can I have a meaningful conversation with myself?

"Five…"

"Four…"

"Three…"

"Two…"

"One…"

I am a wave. Alone, but in a sea of waves that all look the same, just following the motions. Constantly reaching out for something but always being pulled back.

"Keep counting. Feel your muscles start to melt as you become more relaxed. Focus on the numbers. Remove all thought. It's time to face our loneliness. Think about how you feel. Think about all those times you've felt alone. You are now face to face with your loneliness."

I can't follow along. I see nothing sitting in front of me. I am a moving wave that is unable to see the path in front of me.

"What do you feel when you look at your loneliness? What do you want to say to it? Remember to keep breathing. You might start to feel tense, but remember to keep breathing."

What does loneliness look like when someone pictures it? A large, black, amorphous object? Do they see their reflection? Do they see Gilbert Gottfried? This exercise has done nothing but make me feel empty and question who I am. Why is it I am incapable of imagining anything anymore?

"I want you to imagine yourself confronting your loneliness. Imagine all those things that make you feel unhappy and sad. I want you to slowly let them dissolve. Tell your loneliness you don't want to be that way anymore. Let each unhappy thought or experience dissolve. Your mind wants to change, you want to feel different.

"As your loneliness dissolves, think about what you can replace it with. What feelings, what experiences can you replace it with that will make you feel happy? Spending more time with friends? Meaningful conversation? It might require effort, but you can change. You can feel loved."

I can't quite bring myself to believe that love exists. If it did, a majority of the Earth's population wouldn't be as miserable as they are. Friends, parents, the couple at the mall, everyone argues constantly – what's the rationale behind it? One true love? Someone who understands you enough to always argue with you? Consistently forgotten in the concept of finding your true love is the fact that in addition to understanding you, you must understand them. Of course, it should seem implicit that if you are their true love, and they are your true love, that you both must hold an understanding of each other – but most people don't fantasize about love's duality. We are a society of self-serving jerk offs. Our true love must understand us, end of story. At no point should we have to change or make the effort to come to a mutual understanding. So what is my problem then, am I not willing to understand someone or change? Or am I dodging being understood, not just by others but by myself.

"I want you to start to appreciate yourself. Feel comfortable with yourself. Once you start to feel comfortable with yourself, you can start to increase your contact with others. Have meaningful conversations. You are not alone."

Maybe love is just finding someone you enjoy making compromises for. Love is finding someone who you don't mind changing your hopes and dreams for, because you realize that you've mutually developed new hopes and dreams. Physical attraction is important, and I think most people have a tendency to confuse love with the desire to fuck someone so badly that you will temporarily make sacrifices. Once you've gotten what you wanted, you become unattached and stuck in a relationship you have no real desire to be in. You wonder, *how did I ever love this person?* Well, the answer is simple: you never did. Am I better off to not be attached at all?

"Think about all the conversations you've had with people this week. How many people have you connected with? How many people could you have connected with on a deeper level?"

Some people just settle for the first person to pay any attention to them. They are so enamoured by the attention of another person that they convince themselves that they are feeling love. Maybe if we weren't constantly saturated with the belief that we need to find love, we'd stop finding it around every corner. We lose sight of the fact that love is self-sacrifice, and continually look to others to sacrifice for us.

"There are so many places to connect with people. Did any strangers greet you? Did you talk to a store clerk? Did you share a conversation with a coworker? Close relationships can grow from all kinds of contact."

I am starting to get the impression that I might just be an asshole. What is the point of this great inner debate. Can I just let go? I've made myself judge, looking for wrongdoing in everyone else when really I am just as much a perpetrator.

If put to rest my angry and judgmental thoughts, would I be left with anything to think?

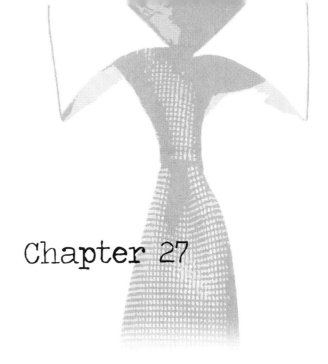

Chapter 27

I've spent the past few days stowed away in my apartment. My recent interactions with people have led me to try an extended stay away from any sort of social entanglements. At first I was invigorated by the thought of disconnecting myself completely from the outside world. No morning commute, work, internet, phone, email, or news: just peace. Time passed with ease the first night.

In the morning I found my spirit drained of any enthusiasm. Despite having all the time in the world to sleep in, I couldn't help but wake up early. The past two days have been completely the same. I wake up early, but don't have the energy to leave my bed. I just lay there enveloped in my own languor. Eventually I manage to stumble into the kitchen with my shoulders curled forward, barely able to find the strength to lift my head up. I drink several glasses of water, and like a good boy I swallow my pill. Hard to tell if the medication is killing my spirit, or if being alone wasn't as invigorating as I had previously believed it to be. Or perhaps my subconscious mind is trying to digest the fact that *this is my life*. There is no grand adventure awaiting me. If I simply stop leaving my apartment, the world will continue undeterred without me. What I've learned from my quiet introspection is that we are responsible for our own excitement. I suppose that is the appeal of drugs: instant self-gratification and excitement.

To break the pattern of listlessness I decide to go to the park. With two days of solitude under my belt I choose to re-enter the world with a quiet walk. With each pill my distaste for people erodes, and I find I am behaving more and more like someone else. The constant inner dialogue of critiquing the world and everyone in it stops. In the absence of cynical narration, I am actually hoping I might meet someone on my walk today. I want my world to collide with a stranger's. I want conversation and connection to flourish and take me to somewhere less miserable.

Here I am sitting on the ground just to the left of a nature trail. I'm greeting a passersby with a sweaty glare and flash of eagerness.

Nothing. My world remains in isolation as strangers safely navigate around me and my spurious smile.

If ever there was a moment where my skewed expectations of reality were crushed completely, it would be right now. I've read too many books and watched too many movies. Here I sit, expecting someone interesting to just run into me, and after a few minutes of conversation we fall madly in love. I expect something *new* to happen with my life simply because I am here waiting and hoping. The longer I wait, the less likely it seems I will fall in love or get whisked away into an unexpected adventure. To everyone in this park I am just some guy staring down anyone who walks by on the nature trail. I am sweaty and annoying.

What is it like to be someone else? Someone other people gravitate towards?

I see an attractive woman walking towards me with her dog, an overweight Chow Chow. Maybe it's not overweight, it's hard to tell what's just fur fluffing out from the dog and what might actually be fat. Regardless, the dog is happily wagging its tail and enthralled by everything it sees. A dandelion, a squirrel, a baby in a stroller – anything the dog sees causes it immediate excitement. Dogs seem to share the same curious nature as infants. The world is full of wonder, and they just love touching, smelling, and feeling everything new that comes their way. Eventually the infant matures and learns to not get so excited about the minor details life offers, but a dog's sense of wonder never fades. The woman walking the dog seems to get annoyed every time the dog veers off the walking path to smell a tree or look at something. She jerks his leash and yells at him, as if the dog has done something wrong. I guess the dog isn't the one going for a walk; the woman is, and she is dragging the dog along while she power walks the calories away. Poor dog, he only gets one hour a day to explore the world outside of the house but he is completely robbed of the opportunity by an overbearing owner. I'm watching the woman as she walks closer to me. Despite the crude way she is treating man's best friend, I still wouldn't mind if the next ten minutes played out like a John Cusack movie. She stops to talk to me, writes her name in a book at the public library, and I end up back at her place holding a stereo over my head. The woman is only a few feet away from me now but she doesn't seem too interested in me. I look directly at her and smile. I am fully prepared to say hello. She keeps walking closer, and is now right beside me. Her dog trots towards me and may just be the first living thing excited to meet me today. Our chance encounter is abruptly ended by the owner tugging on the dog's leash followed by a verbal scolding unleashed on the dog for pursuing its impulsive desire to greet me. The woman has now walked past me, and my hello has now turned into a low whisper,

"Let your dog enjoy his fucking walk."

The woman looks back at me, she seems upset by my comment. We finally make eye contact, but instead of a John Cusack movie, it's more likely to play out like a Steve Buscemi movie. No girls ever fall in love with Steve Buscemi … they just seem to get creeped out by him. The woman rolls her eyes and walks out of my life forever. Yet my words must have made some sort of impression on her, because in the distance I can now see her waiting patiently while her dog sniffs a tree.

I had been in a good mood. The smile on my face is slowly fading as my head sinks lower and lower into my chest. I'm no longer able to make eye contact with strangers in the park, it just feels like I am getting in the way of people enjoying their afternoon. I pull out my orange container and discretely open the lid. *This must be how homeless people feel.* I pop another pill and start to think about Mary. For whatever reason, Mary seems to tolerate me. The only reason I can come up with is alcohol, so it makes sense to me that I should abandon the park for the nearest pub. With luck, there will be some local patrons I can endear myself to by drinking excessively in the afternoon. After all, no one likes to get afternoon drunk alone.

The first pub to happen upon my path is a rather bland-looking place. A plain brick building surrounded by equally bland brick buildings, at the centre of an old decaying strip of shops all with the same menacing aura of tedium.

Floyd's.

Not a very creative name. I'm standing under the glowing – well, more like decaying light of the sign. It's covered in dirt collected through years of neglect. I imagine that the guy who's neglecting the sign has a father named Floyd, and Floyd neglected him as a child by spending his time at his pub trying to make ends meet. Now that he is all grown up, Floyd Junior has dispelled the illusion that father knows best. His father was more of a myth than a role model and now his disappointment is reflected in the continued disregard of his father's name hanging over the main entrance. My first impression of Floyd's after walking through the main entrance is underwhelming. Floyd's is beyond ordinary. I can't find a single detail about this place stands out or is worth remembering.

When you're feeling especially ordinary, an establishment lacking any sort of unique character can provide quite a homey sensation.

Breathing seems easier and somehow my muscles just feel more relaxed. In here, I don't have to be anything but the maladjusted human being that I am. The walls are coated with self-loathing, and the foundation was built on complacency.

I am at ease.

All the windows seem to be propped open by chunks of wood. Either they don't have air conditioning, or they are indifferent towards the escape of their artificially-birthed cold air. Mankind has a seemingly endless supply of cold air just waiting to be created.

Walking towards the bar I do my best to appear nonchalant. I'm unaccustomed to adjusting my behaviour to fit in – must be the pills. The warning label has overlooked the sudden urge to be accepted by others as a side effect, which seems counterintuitive for an anti-anxiety medication if you ask me.

There's several empty seats at the bar and the tables in the pub are more or less vacant. I guess not many people feel as ordinary as I do today. It would be an incredible slight to social protocol if I took a table to drink by myself, so the bar is my only real option to sit. The whole purpose of a bar in a pub is to accommodate loners in the most comforting way possible. It's like a playpen for adults. You enter alone, and as a result of proximity you're drawn into conversation with a stranger beside you.

The best way to avoid looking lonely when you're walking into a pub alone is to avoid making eye contact with anyone. Find your seat and move towards it with an unwavering sense of purpose. If you spend too much time looking around and questioning what seat you should take, you will come off as nervous. If someone happens to catch your gaze you can flash a casual smile, just be sure you immediately bring your attention back to something more pressing, like ordering your first drink. Look at me, I'm in control.

"Bullshit!" The old man to my left tries to waft away the smell of bullshit coming from the television above the bar.

"Fair is fair works both ways. Ignorant little shit." The old man turns towards me, and slowly eyes me. Slouching, the old man puts his elbow on the bar and leans his head against the palm of his hand. "Not enough money to raise minimum wage, but plenty of money to keep Scrooge McDuck sailing comfortably in his yacht."

I reply with some sort of affirming grunt and nod of my head. The bartender interrupts just in time.

"I'll take the strongest beer you've got."

"One of those afternoons, huh." The bartender's evocative statement spurs a wave of self-loathing throughout my body. I loathe this situation and the disapproving glare of the bartender. Can't I order a strong drink in the middle of the afternoon, without being judged?

"Just looking to save time." I smile.

The bartender chuckles as he plunks down a glass containing some sort of dark brown liquor. I can't inhale this drink fast enough. I'm uneasy, and not for the regular reasons. I actually have the urge to converse with the man to my left. This isn't like me. Normally I drink to overcome my desire to avoid social interaction, but today I am drinking to manage my inclination to engage in friendly banter with this stranger.

"Ya want a smoke, bud?" With his head still resting on his hand, the man to my left extends a pack of cigarettes and raises his right eyebrow. I look at him and use a gesture to signal that I am not interested in his offer. His hand remains extended with the cigarette package, and he remains positioned comfortably leaning on his hand and slouching at the bar. He motions the package towards me, scrunching his face slightly.

"I don't smoke. Those things will kill you," I explain.

"Now that's the point, isn't it?"

The man lifts his arm from off the bar and slugs down the last of his pint.

"Who the fuck wants to live forever? You know what the downside of immortality is? You gotta spend eternity trying to entertain yourself. I prefer to gamble with socially acceptable forms of suicide. Maybe these things kill me, maybe they don't. They help me pass the time, anyway." The man slides out of his bar stool and walks towards the door, dancing with a cigarette in hand as he weaves between tables and patrons.

"Argh," disapproval rings loudly from the lady sitting to my right. "You're so full of yourself. Don't listen to him, dear, he thinks he's a poet." The old lady doesn't even take her eyes of her drink, which is some sort of cocktail in a tall glass that she's stabbing at with a straw.

"If you know anything about poets, they always think people care about the bullshit they have to say."

"Don't we all think that?"

"Come again?" Looking unimpressed, the old lady turns towards me.

"Don't we all assume everyone cares what we have to share? I mean what's the point of half the conversations we have. Some people spend an entire conversation just looking for a way to weave themselves into the narrative. Some people don't even listen to the other person."

"Boy, you sound bitter for your age. You get dumped by your sweetheart or something?"

"No." I take a big drink from whatever the hell is in my glass. Wincing from the awful taste, I manage to gurgle out a hasty reply. "I've always been bitter, I suppose."

"You've always been bitter. Were you bitter as a little boy, complaining to all the other little boys in the sandbox about your problems?"

Spinning the glass between my fingers, I try to call back a moment from my childhood. What's the last happy memory I can remember? Nothing. Blank. Pressing my eyelids closed as hard as I can, I try to force a memory to appear. Still nothing. Did I even have a childhood? Of course I did, but I can't seem to picture anything. Before I open my eyes and all but give up, I see a faint mental image of myself as a young child. I'm crouched inside some sort of bush in an opening just big enough to crawl into. I seem to be smiling, and though I can't quite recall exactly what I am doing hiding in that bush,

I recall a feeling of freedom. I am free of worry or care. I *was* free of worry and care … I was happy. I can remember that now. I'm packed up tight in a one-piece snowsuit, laying in a pile of snow and looking up to the sky through a hole in the bush. The sky is an endless sea of blue that just seems to go on forever. My arms are laid out straight against my sides, my hands are kept warm by my mitts, and my body is enveloped in the body heat trapped in my snowsuit. I can feel the cold air on my face in sharp contrast to the rest of my body. I watch quietly as each breath slowly plumes out of my mouth and disappears into nothing as it mixes with the air. The only sounds I can hear are caused by a small gust of wind pushing through the bush, rattling every branch and blowing the snow in the open field behind me. There's something about this serene moment of solitude that makes me feel more relaxed than I've ever been. I'd give *anything* to feel this way again. The cold air on my face quickly turns to room temperature as I open my eyes. I think I've just come to an understanding about what makes a drug user an addict. All the stories I've heard of addicts going to extreme means just to get one more hit somehow seem justified now.

"I guess you're right. Somewhere along the way my thoughts got a little too busy, just sort of forgot what it felt like to be a kid."

The old lady smirks for a few seconds, downs her drink, and tells me, "You should work on that."

I watch the lady rise from her chair, grab her purse, and make her way out of Floyd's. I don't follow her movement out of the bar, instead I find my gaze fixated on her now empty chair. My mind is running through our conversation. All her words, all the emotions felt in my memory, they are so vivid right now. This chair has become a gateway into another world, a world that I can only hear and feel, yet it seems so real. My journey into another world ends abruptly after the sound of an arm hitting the bar me rips me from my chair-induced introspection. The arm belongs to the old man who has triumphantly announced his return with a forceful blow to the bar. He reeks of cigarettes and probably wants to talk to someone. I figure I might as well since there are no other candidates for random interaction within my line of sight. The young man a few seats down from us is the only other occupant of the bar and he seems far too engrossed with his phone to take any notice of anything that isn't his phone or beverage. I feel calm about the situation. Is my serenity because they're strangers, or because I'm medicated?

"So you just get your heart broke by your lady?"

"No ... why does everyone keep saying that?"

The old man looks around the room in an exaggerated manner. "Who's everyone?"

"Well, you and the lady who left. So I guess it's just the small sample of people at this bar that at the moment make up my reality."

"Did that guy say anything?" the old man motions to the kid down from us. He's still fingering his phone and takes no notice of us.

"No, I don't think he's looked up from that thing since I've been here."

"Well, you're in a pub." The man motions with his hands, as if in some grand gesture he's revealing an unseen world to me.

"Alone." He brings his hands back to the bar table and forces his face to a frown.

"It's early afternoon and you order the stiffest drink you can get your hands on." This man must be some sort of stage actor, he has a knack for hamming up every gesture and expression to help make his point. He may also just be drunk.

"Can't I get drunk in the afternoon without a precipitating bout of heartbreak, or is there some rule I'm not aware of?"

"You can get drunk whenever you want. Just trying to help a stranger, no offence intended." The man puts his hands up and gestures apologetically.

"Why?"

Signalling the bartender for a new beer, the old man looks me right in the eye. "Why what?"

"Why try and help a stranger, what would you get out of it?"

The old man snorts and takes a drink from his fresh beer. "Well, maybe your generation has their collective heads stuck up their assess, but that's really all we got in life."

"Helping strangers is all we got?"

"No, didn't I just tell you to get your head out of your ass?" The old man laughs and takes another drink before turning his body completely towards me.

"Each other. When it comes down to it, all we have are the people around us. Maybe if everyone tried being nice to each other for a change, this planet wouldn't be such a terrible place to be. That's the gist of what some guy tried to tell us a few thousand years ago, but we hammered him to a tree for it."

There's a drawn out lull in our conversation as we both attend to our drinks.

"Look, you're not one of those sob cases, are you? Always complaining about how bad you got it?"

"I generally avoid talking about my personal life." I shrug my left shoulder and avoid making any eye contact. I'm suddenly on the defensive.

"Good. I swear, being sad has become the hip way to be. Everyone arguing about who has it worse and writing sad songs about it. Fuck my life, everyone says. Being sad is easy. It's like a default setting. Being happy takes effort and determination. You can't be happy if you're lazy. You gotta work for it."

"Well..." putting both my hands on the bar, I turn slightly towards the old man, "I guess it's just hard to find anything to be happy about."

The old man shakes his head. "You're alive, aren't you? You have a place to live, all five senses working in proper order, and full use of your mind. Life is what you want to make it. If you want to be sad because you didn't turn out to be a stud, well, you're not going to find anything better at the bottom of that glass. I think there's a pill for that now."

I find myself laughing for the first time. A legitimate unbridled laughter. The irony and truth in the old man's statement mixed with alcohol just seem funny.

"What's at the bottom of your beer?"

The old man smirks, "Whatever the hell I want there to be." He slams back the rest of his beer and leans closer to me with an eyebrow raised. "Let's see if I can find some more." Sensing the impending need for a drink, the bartender slides another beer over to the old man. He continues, "Look, kid. You just gotta learn to like yourself. You're probably never going to like your life, so just try liking yourself. Then maybe you can extend the effort to liking other people."

"What if I don't like myself?"

The old man looks frustrated for the first time. "Look, I'm not a fortune cookie. Trust me, you'll have a lot less worries if you can figure out how to like yourself. You're off to a good start: you've taken yourself out and bought yourself a nice stiff drink. Maybe get yourself drunk, take yourself back to your apartment, and ravage yourself." The old man laughs and takes another drink.

"Those news reports, or the fact that my son over here hasn't said a word or looked up from his phone since we've been here don't get me down because I like myself enough to be OK with the bad stuff. My failures, faults, all the things I wish I had done and said. Of course all that shit disappoints me and I wish I could go back and change things, but I like myself enough to focus on what I'm going to do next. There's always a chance for redemption in the next move, you know? No need to hate myself or beat myself up about the past. I save that for when I repeat mistakes."

I stammer out an approximation of a compliment that is swirling around my head. "Pretty progressive of you."

"Our lives never turn out the way we want them to, if they did, it would probably be pretty boring anyway." The man takes a large drink, pausing for a moment to casually lean to the side and burp. "No challenge. No adversity. So instead of focusing on all the bad shit, try doing two things: like yourself, and stop thinking that everything shitty that happens has anything to do with who you are. Shit happens. And you know what shit is, right? Fertilizer. Take all that shit that happens, and use it to grow something useful."

The old man stands up and looks down at me breathing hard. "Buck up."

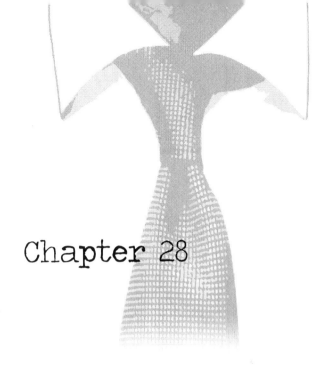

Chapter 28

Wandering around a convenience store and drinking from an unpaid water bottle, I'm in a desperate fight against dehydration and the pounding of my brain against my skull. Afternoon drinks don't bring delight. I picked out the largest water bottle I could find and now I'm exploring the colourful array of snacks laid out on shelves for my convenience. My nose brings me down an aisle of freshly baked pastries, full of rich sinful aromas dancing all around me. The smell is simply tantalizing. Even now, minutes later, I'm still intoxicated from the scent. My mouth is watering as I fantasize about all the textures and tastes I'm denying myself out of some personal philosophy built on discipline. Really, my philosophy is built on vanity and the overwhelming need to be in control. I'm shaking my head from side to side, trying to convince myself to say no, but I can feel new horizons starting to open in my mind. The sweet sugary scent of the sinful donuts in front of me is stimulating my dopamine receptors. I need a fix. I want a fix. Maybe this is exactly what Tim wants me to be doing, giving up control and opening myself up to living in the moment. Giving in to impulse. Looking around the aisle to ensure I'm alone, I move toward the bin holding the donuts and reach in. I've no intention of letting others see me eat this donut. It will be my dark secret. Baby steps, I tell myself as I pull the donut close and turn my body into a corner between the bins and wall. I close my eyes to heighten the experience and make my move. My lips press against the donut when my concentration is broken.

"What do you mean, *you're out!?*" Shouting pulls me from my slightly sexual encounter with a donut. Disbelief in the store's supply chain management process has gotten the best of someone today. A quick bite goodbye before I toss the donut to the floor and kick it under a shelf. I'm not sure if I just maintained control or lost control by allowing shame to guide my actions. Either way my mouth is swimming in flavour as I walk towards the shouting to see what all the commotion is about. Wiping icing from my mouth, I pull up to the checkout where a man is aggressively pointing to an item on a flyer and huffing, and puffing, and blowing this department store in.

The clerk shrugs his shoulders apologetically, "I'm sorry, *sir*. We sold out within our first day."

"*You* sold out!" The man responds as if the clerk had gone out of his way to personally ensure stock sold out. "The flyer just came out yesterday, how do you sell out?"

"Well, we had fifty in stock. Then customers came in and purchased all fifty items. Now we're out." The clerk lays the sarcasm on thick.

"How do you not have any in the back?"

"Well, the back isn't some magical room with wardrobes that let us reach into other worlds to resupply our shelves. It's a closet with limited quantities of stock."

Flicking donut out of my front teeth with my tongue I can't help but chuckle at the clerk's mockery. This kid's got a bright future.

"Well, when are you getting *more* in! I should be able to pay the sale price and pick it up when it comes in!"

The clerk sighs. "Look, we're just a convenience store. I'm just a cashier. You're talking about saving two dollars on a case of pop. They might be in tomorrow. Maybe it'll take two days. I don't know."

"You don't know."

"I don't know."

"Maybe tomorrow?"

"Maybe tomorrow."

"But also maybe in two days?"

"Yes, maybe in two days."

"Can someone call me to let me know they come in?"

Jesus, you're trying to buy cases of pop. Go to another store and pay the extra two dollars.

"We're just a convenience store." The clerk ensures careful and slow enunciation of each word. "We don't call customers about how much cola product is in stock."

"Unbelievable! What kind of customer service is this!"

"The kind you get at a small convenience store?" Credit to the clerk for persevering through this conversation. What should have been a simple, *we're out of stock,* conversation has mutated into some sort of live theatre production about a man who just doesn't get it. It's taken five minutes of back and forth dialogue to motivate the man to storm out of the store with a chip on his shoulder. In his eyes, he deserves to get those cans of pop at the mediocre sale price. The world owes it to him. Doesn't everyone know that he is the single most important person in his world?

The idea that we are special and unique is regurgitated by anyone who has a significant impact on formative development. You grow up and your parents tell you at every chance that you're their special little person. You go to school and your teachers enable you with entire lessons about how special and unique you are. Entire television shows, songs, and storybooks are made just to tell you that you are beautiful and unique just the way you are. Don't bother trying to make yourself a better person or anything because you're perfect! Don't feel like you need to earn anything. You're perfect and you deserve things just because of who you are!

It's not until you get a job that someone finally informs you just how regular you are. You might even discover you're actually inept. A total fuck up. I suppose if you really wanted to look at things positively, your ineptitude is what makes you special and unique: no one can fuck up simple tasks like you can.

We have a way of perceiving the universe as made just for us, completely ignoring the other million species that exist on the planet. Aiding us in our ignorance is the idea that each tree, animal, and blade of grass was made for our disposal by some god. Justification for just about anything other than masturbation and gay marriage can be found in the Bible. It would be a significant blow to humanity to discover that our existence was the result of happenstance, the spark of life ignited in a pile of primordial goo, just because. The mistake of life has been spiraling out of control ever since that first single cell organism burst onto the scene and now that life has achieved consciousness in humans, it finally has a mechanism to feel special.

Shifting my weight on my feet, I erupt into a spastic rhythm of stretching that ends with me reaching into my pocket to grab the little orange container of pills. The Bible has a story about the Jews wandering through the desert for forty years, surviving off nothing but miraculously appearing manna. I'm unclear what manna really was or where it came from, but these pills are my manna. I'm lost in a shitty job with my people for the next forty years and I think this manna might be the only thing that will get me through it. I pull out one of the round little pills from its container and hold it between my index finger and thumb. I pause to stare at the pill before slipping it into my mouth and swallowing. With my eyes closed and head tilted back, I hear the clerk,

"So, you going to pay for that or..."

Opening my eyes I'm immediately drawn to the glare of the clerk as he eyes up the water bottle in my hand.

"Right. Sorry. Forgot where I was for a minute." Nervous laughter.

"Mhmm." The cashier reaches out as I pass him the half-drunken water bottle from my hand.

"Thirsty?"

"Extremely. Didn't think that guy would stop, so I got a little premature."

With a slight grin, the clerk retorts, "Hopefully that's the only time you're premature."

I could take this as an insult, but I realize he is actually being friendly with me. Amazing. Just minutes ago he was getting shit from a customer, and now he is making friendly banter with me. "You don't seem to let assholes like that last guy get you down."

"Hakuna Matata, man."

I raise my eyebrow, "*Lion King*?"

"You bet your ass. That means no worries. It'd be a pretty shitty life if I worried about all the assholes in it, so hakuna matata."

"No worries. You make it sound easy."

"That's 'cause it is." The clerk pulls out a stick of gum from his smock and in one sweeping motion slides the stick into his mouth. Maybe I'm on a hidden camera and this is a Juicy Fruit commercial.

"This has been quite an enlightening water purchase. You have a good one."

Walking out of the store, I think about what the cashier said. Is life that simple? If I want to be happy, I can just be happy? Why don't I just stop worrying and relax?

It's at this thought I find myself slumped on a curb with a growing urge to give Jeff a shout. No doubt he is out with Steve talking about something stupid, entangled in some meaningless spell of a gabfest. A small part of me shudders at the thought of Friday nightlife, but that quiet indignation is so small that it becomes overpowered by a new feeling. I've got a new desire to talk about nothing and to be in the presence of others. I look down at the orange container still in my hand and wonder if it's possible to change who you are. It's possible that we are at the mercy of biological secretions. X amount of testosterone plus Y amount of serotonin equals you. If we are the accumulation of chemicals, depending on how static that balance of chemicals is, we may have more than one personality hidden within us. One personality has a numerical supremacy over the rest, but take a tiny little pill and the equation changes. The balance of power shifts to allow a friendlier personality to take over. I suppose my arts degree won't help me arrive at any more insightful conclusion than this.

Do I know who I want to be, or just who I don't want to be?

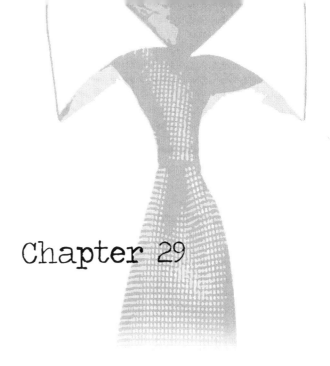

Chapter 29

"You know, sometimes it feels like you are repeating yourself. You have a great way of analyzing the world, but I want to know, how do you really feel? And I mean feel, not what do you think, but what are you feeling?"

"I feel frustrated."

"That's good. Let's focus on that for right now. You feel frustrated."

"That's right. I'm frustrated."

Tim remains in his chair, looking at me. Tim can see me. He's not looking through me, he's not looking down on me, he is seeing me. It doesn't seem like there's any pressure for Tim to speak. I feel like a spotlight is beaming down on me and the attention is making me sweat and feel anxious.

"I'm frustrated because I feel stuck."

Tim hones in on one word and repeats it. "Stuck."

"Yah. Stuck. Like I'm trapped in my own life. I have no choices anymore. Work. Eat. Sleep."

"No choices anymore. So you had choices once. But then something changed. What's different?"

"I grew up."

"What choices are you no longer able to make now that you've grown up?"

Silence.

"If you once again had your ability to make choices, what would you choose to do?"

"Well. I guess I probably wouldn't wake up at 6 am, every Monday to Friday."

"So you'd sleep in. Anything else you'd be doing differently?"

"I probably wouldn't even go to work."

Tim nods his head. "So where would you go, what would you do instead?"

I laugh nervously. I'm starting to realize I've never really thought about *what else* I would be doing. It's so easy to focus on what I don't want to do that I never give much thought to what I'd rather be doing. "I'd like to read more."

"Mhhmmm." Tim hums as he nods his head. I feel the urge to continue brainstorming.

"I'd have control over my day."

Tim crosses his legs. "Control. How so?"

"It's never up to me what I do all day. I always have something to do. Always busy. Always tired. Why the hell am I always busy? What am I always doing? Whatever I'm told. I drone my way through each day and I just want to stop. I want to do what I want."

"You have no control over your day. Perhaps that's why control over your emotions is so important to you." Silence. Tim might be right, but I'm not ready to admit it. Maybe if I don't say anything we can just stare at each other until we run out of time.

"I'm curious," Tim keeps pressing, "if you were doing what you wanted, you had total control, what would you be doing?"

"What would I be doing?" I stew in the question for a few minutes. I'm drawing blanks, unable to articulate any sort of ideas about what I want. "Maybe I'd sit at home and dissolve."

"And that would give you a sense of control?"

"Yes. I'd be doing something on my own terms. Dissolving might not necessarily be an ideal outcome, but staying home would be nice."

Tim stays on the offensive, setting me up for a knockout blow. "So what is stopping you from making that choice?"

"Bills. Daily need to eat. I need some kind of income."

Another blow leaves me vulnerable for the kill. "And you can't find income from any source other than what you are currently doing?"

Silence.

"I get the sense that the choice you have made, the choice to continue in your current job and go through the motions, is what you are stuck in." Tim has me on the ropes. One more shot and I'm finished.

"Is it possible," Tim closes his hands together and brings them close to his face – it's possible he is discreetly picking his nose – "that you are avoiding making different choices? Changing careers, calling in sick, picking up hobbies, finding more time to read?"

Desperate, I spit my last breath in defence. "Why would I avoid choosing to do anything?"

"Interesting question. Why would you?" Did Tim just grab my hand and hit me with it? *Stop hitting yourself. Stop hitting yourself.*

"Isn't avoiding a choice? I'm intentionally choosing not to find a different job or read more."

"You've *decided* not to find a different job or do anything about how depressed you've become."

"Yes." I pause. "No." Shaking my head. "Who said I was depressed?"

"You never said it, but it is what I feel when I hear you share. When I said you are avoiding choice, and you stated that you are intentionally not making any changes, it felt to me as if you've fallen in a hole and given up on getting out."

"So now I'm in a hole." I'm trying to brush Tim off. I'm not very convincing.

"What I mean is, on one hand you *want* something different out of life. To be less busy. To have more free time. To have more say in how you direct your energy. On the other hand, you don't want a worse life. Less money. More stress. Uncertainty. So you're not sure if you should get out of the hole. It's kept you safe so far. Is that fair?"

Tim really doesn't like buried emotions. He just keeps digging away and he's got a good map. "That's fair."

"So that brings us back to the idea that you want change but you don't want it to be worse. You feel stuck." Tim no longer looks proud of himself. He looks like a guy trying to help another human. It's more likely that Tim has always been trying to help me, and I've simply stopped trying to find ill-intent in every intonation.

"Stuck. Like a mouse in a glue trap. It hurts when I try and wriggle my way out of this, sticky bullshit."

"A mousetrap. That's a good analogy, gets across that feeling that maybe you've been tricked by the bait laying on the trap." Tim's managed to make me sound more clever than I actually am. "So, you've stopped trying to wriggle. It doesn't hurt when you're not fighting."

No words, I just nod.

"And so, you avoid making choices to avoid the pain of wriggling out of that trap."

The knockout blow. I can't even argue with Tim. What is there to argue with?

"So, you are saying I should quit my job?"

"I haven't really said anything. I'm just helping to clarify. Is quitting something you might want to do?"

"Yes and no…" I sigh. What more could Tim want from me?

"It's the mousetrap. You could quit, but that might be a terrible choice. You might not end up with the same income or security. It might lead to pain and another trap. It could also be a great choice and lead to escape. Is there another choice?"

I express that I'm taken aback by his question by leaning back as far as I can in my chair. "Another choice, like get a second job? Hypnotize myself to like my current job?" Here comes the cynicism.

"Those are other choices. What I'm wondering is, have you considered that you might be able to look for another job without actually quitting your current one? You could apply, interview, and accept before quitting your current job. You could look into night classes or training, map out a route to a new career."

"I see your point, Tim."

"I'm glad you see that there are choices still to be made. That maybe you aren't as stuck as you think and maybe there is no mouse trap."

"And so what is there?"

"The normal feelings and discomfort that come with living. That little voice inside that panics at every turn and tells you to just stay put. Don't put yourself in harm's way. But when you do that, you're not really living. You're just lying still and letting life pass by. To live is to hurt, to be unhappy, and to fail. Yet, living is also to be happy, to learn, and to have success. Life's not a zero sum game."

I exhale deeply and lean back into my chair. Several minutes pass and Tim remains stoic as I process everything that has happened. Tim only waits a few minutes before he picks me up and tosses me back on the ropes.

"There's something else that I always feel when we talk. It is a bit more difficult to share this, it is a kind of … feeling, or attitude I hear when you talk."

Tim seems to be waiting for my permission to continue, so I nod my head to prod him on.

"A lot of times when you speak, I get the sense from what you say that you don't want other people in your life. Based on our relationship and our conversations, I feel you are steering us away from any sort of conversation that may leave you vulnerable. That may allow me to get a sense of who you are and for us to build a bond."

For whatever reason I am still nodding. I can't seem to find any words to fit the moment.

"I wonder. Is that what others experience when they are with you? Is that something you've felt yourself?"

"I uh…" If I'd been protecting myself against Tim, clearly, I failed. "I do feel a distance between me and others."

"A distance? I'd like to hear more about that."

"Distance. It's like when I am with people, I'm not really with them, as if there is some sort of distance."

Tim counters, "How would you describe the distance: physically distant, or intellectually distant?"

"Physical or intellectual … I guess I would have to vote for the latter. I can't seem to relate to what other people talk about. What they spend their time focused on. It all seems so … I don't know … just … distant, like we're not living in the same world."

"You are better off alone because other people aren't up to your intellectual standards and don't share your values." Uppercut to the jaw. Dirty elbow to the head.

"Yes." Tim's comment gives me pause. The way I feel sounds so much more ridiculous when someone else says it out loud to me. I don't sound like a nice person.

"How's that working out for you?"

"Hmm?" I know what Tim is saying, but I don't want to face myself anymore. I don't like who I've met.

"Has isolation brought you what you want?"

"I used to think so."

"You're not sure anymore. We all need people in our lives. Friends at work, family, loved ones. It's OK to break down the walls and close the distance."

"It's how I've defined myself for so long. I don't know who I'd be if I didn't." *Have I ever really been clear on who I am, or am I just clear on who I am not?*

"That's a good question. Can you choose to change how you define yourself?"

"Back to choice I see, Tim."

"That's right." Tim smiles. "I hear you say you don't know how else you'd define yourself, not that you *can't* redefine yourself. Something to think about is that you can't know anything with any sort of certainty. Life unfolds and you can either respond by making choices that push you forward, or you can stay stuck in indecision. Avoid taking responsibility and deflect onto others everything that you failed to do."

"Tim, that has to be the most pointed thing you've said to me. I think I am starting to like the way you think. So you're saying I should quit my job and go on some sort of personal journey to find myself?" I find myself resorting to old barriers: I am becoming closed-off and defensive again.

"You tell me."

"You're the counsellor, why don't you try counseling?" I immediately regret the words that come out of my mouth, but I can't seem to control myself. I am reacting, I am wounded, and I am trying to protect myself.

"You're right. I am the counsellor, and it seems like you are constantly trying to avoid taking responsibility for making a decision in your life. You already know what you want me to say, so why don't you just tell me? What is it you want me to tell you?"

"I'm sorry." Two simple words that I don't use often enough. "You're right. Even now I'm trying to avoid this conversation and blame you. I need to take responsibility. Buck up."

"So, what's stopping you? If we accept that there is no mousetrap, what is stopping you?"

I suddenly find myself laughing. Tim's right. There is nothing stopping me. There never has been. There's a small victory to be had in being able to laugh at your own misery, especially laughing at the sudden realization that I am my own problem. Not the world. Not the people in it.

I think, therefore I am full of excuses.

What now?

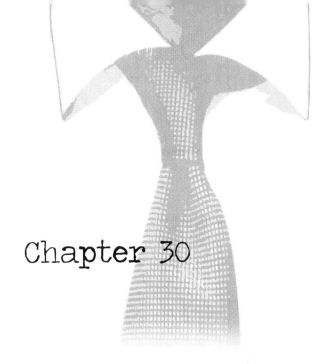

Chapter 30

If I had a slightly better life, what would it look like? What would I be like?
Nothing.

Good questions that I have no idea how to answer. I can hear Tim in my mind, challenging me to think about what I would actually want out of myself. Out of work. Out of life. It feels alien to ruminate on change as opposed to problems, as if I have stepped into a world of puppy dogs and rainbows, or worse, a Tony Robbins infomercial. Positive thoughts and good attitude about walking over hot coals won't change anything, but neither will a cycle of re-digesting disappointment. Self-improvement is getting over yourself, coming to terms with what you're doing wrong, and doing something about it. I am starting to understand that maybe it isn't the world improving I should worry about, rather it is myself improving I should focus on. I can't change work or people around me, but I can change. What remains is figuring out just what the hell I need to change and how. I might need a different set of eyes.

It's Friday night and I decide to throw on a movie. Two hours to suspend reality and immerse myself in another world, and yet, despite my valiant efforts to run away, I find I am standing still on a single question.

Why am I so angry?

I created an idea of what life ought to be like, how people should think, act, and feel. Seven billion people on this planet and I believe that somehow I am the only one who gets it. Everyone is stupid and in my way because they don't act or think like me. How can I be so sure about reality? If seven billion people are viewing life unfold on this rock, then that means there are seven billion vantage points from which to observe and form some sort of understanding and meaning. With so many vantage points, whose details should we pay attention to? Is it possible to truly understand without seeing all the angles? Maybe it's a problem to think there is any sort of meaning in life to be discovered in the first place. Shit happens, as Forrest Gump so eloquently put it. After shit happens we seem to focus our attention on creating stories explaining why shit happened, what shit should have happened, or why certain shit ought to happen. We can't tune our minds to play in the moment. Our minds are attuned to the future and the past, always analyzing and weaving narrative where none otherwise exists. Nature doesn't tell stories. We do.

Life would be much simpler if we were more akin to other animals. A dog is given a treat and just enjoys eating it. The dog isn't burdened by the desire to determine the underlying purpose of the treat and what her place in the world is relative to the treat. She doesn't pull back from the treat and question the motives of the hand that feeds. She doesn't worry about where the next treat is coming from or whether other dogs get better treats. She simply receives the treat and enjoys it, revelling in the experience of the moment. I can't recall the last time I lived in the moment, when I truly lived and enjoyed what was unfolding without stepping behind a two-way mirror, watching, and forcing some kind of narrative or explanation behind everything leading up to and following the moment.

If I had a slightly better life, I would be anchored in the moment rather than floating in a sea of rumination. I would focus on what I want to be, not what I want others to be.

What do I want to be?

To be or what not to be ...

Maybe I am overcomplicating this. If I accept that there is no grand purpose or divine narrative being played out, then maybe all I need to want is to be open. Open to the moment. Open to having no control over life, but control over how I respond. Is that freedom?

OK. So this seems like a good place to have arrived.

What now? Instead of feeling better, I almost feel worse. I see an idea of how I want to be, but that's not how I am. I don't know what I expected. Did I think that part of me would just cease to exist and I would suddenly transform into a new person? A better person without any baggage? I'm still dragging my old luggage around the airport, afraid to take anything out because I can't imagine giving anything up. It won't matter what flight I take or where I travel. If I don't let go of something, I'm going to be weighed down and charged for oversized baggage. I need to let go. Let go of my luggage completely and get on a flight unattached and free. Maybe leaving the entire bag is easier than just pulling out a few items. Is it possible to walk away from your past self like that? Is it possible to start over without being grounded by all your worries, habits, and disappointments?

The movie drones on in the background. I haven't the faintest idea what is happening on screen. My heart isn't in it. I want out. Out of this room, out of this state of mind. Almost reflexively I find myself pulling out my cellphone, dialing Jeff, and holding my phone against my ear.

"Hey! What's goin' on?" Jeff is shouting through the phone, likely with one finger in his opposite ear trying hard to hear what is happening. I suppose he never stops to consider that the issue is not with me being unable to hear what he is saying into the microphone located several inches from his mouth, but Jeff being unable to hear me in the loud room where he is currently located. As a result I hold the phone away from my ear and cringe as he tests my decibel threshold.

"Good."

"No shit. Don't get many calls from you on a Friday night. We're down at O'Flaherty's. Make a trip if you want, got the usual crew here."

"Yah, I think I'd like that."

There's a pause on the phone. I think both Jeff and myself are in disbelief about the positive tone and diction I used.

"Alright, well hurry up. We're a few drinks deep, and no one likes being the only sober person in the group."

A thousand clever replies cycle through my mind, but the closer they get to my tongue they just evaporate. I've got nothing left to say, other than a giddy exclamation of,

"Ya!"

Ya. Yahhhh. Yay! Sarcasm rears its ugly head after I hang up, only this time I seem to be the victim of my own thoughts. Fuck me, because I'm going out. I toss the phone on the couch and quickly run to the mirror to inspect my appearance. I want to look good in public – not pristine, but good in a casual, minimalist kind of way. I want the kind of casual, effortless, good look that takes an hour to sculpt. As I change my shirt into something more appropriate for a Friday night, I manage to wrap my thoughts up in a tidy package. It is around the third button from my neck when revelation strikes. *I'm excited to go out.*

I should learn to meditate, I think, as I finish buttoning my shirt. I turn my body to the side to catch a glimpse of my own butt in the mirror. I've spent so much time wondering about Mary's butt that I've hardly ever considered my own. If presented with a lineup of photos, and on each photo was a picture of someone's butt, I have no confidence that I would be able to determine which butt belonged to me. How often do I get a chance to see myself from behind? An uneasy acceptance about my butt is all I manage. Like a prepackaged brownie, it's OK, but you know there are much better brownies out there. Good thing I'll be sitting on it most of the night, or at least engaging people from my anterior point of view.

I grab my keys, swing open my apartment door, and start my ritual of locking it from the outside. A quick flash of my cell phone sitting on my couch where I tossed it hits me. I consider leaving my cell phone and continuing on to O'Flaherty's. The amount of effort needed to rescue it from my couch and return it to my pocket is fairly high, and the return does not seem high enough to warrant retrieval. As I ponder what to do, I think about how I won't be able to fit in without my cell phone; it's like a security blanket for those moments when you find yourself alone in a bar and need something to fiddle with.

"Fuck!" Turning around I plot a course back to my apartment. Funny how much longer the walk seems to get back to my apartment than when I left. Unlocking the deadbolt and door handle, I rush to the couch without even turning the lights on. After a few seconds of groping my anxiety is fanned down to a calm mellow. I've got my security blankey. I can leave my apartment with peace of mind that regardless of where or when it is, I have a way to connect with the world wide web.

It's fairly serendipitous that the moment I step outside of my apartment building I see an empty taxi just waiting for a passenger. Walking towards the taxi I lean down to meet the eyes of the driver sitting in his car with the window open. He honks his horn and waves me over with a grand gesture of his arms. As I pull open the door, I announce my destination.

"You bet." The driver is young and appears to be Slavic. He has a strong accent and a rather small, bulky frame accented by an exceptionally thick moustache. With his heavy accent, he belts out American slang that he probably picked up from television. He's trying to blend in, just like me. I instantly find myself liking this man.

"Busy night?" I try to look interested in his reply by leaning forward in my seat.

"Friday night, man. All the Americans out, looking to get down and waste their money, kill their minds. But that is OK, I make good tips. Party on."

"Ah, I see. So you pick up a lot of assholes then?"

"Oh yah, brother. I drive the night shifts. Young idiots with lots of money, little respect. I work hard for money to live, for my family. I drive around ungrateful Americans who just want to party. If only I could have the money these people have to throw away."

Trying to divert the conversation somewhere less intense, I shift to something other than work. "So what brought you to America?"

"Civil unrest. I didn't want my family caught up in the fighting, fear, and paranoia. I used to be judge, you know, in the regional courts. Now I drive taxis."

"Didn't want to be a judge in America?"

"Ha. You don't accept my education or qualifications here. It's as if you think I presided over pagans in a cave. So I drive taxi."

I sink back into my seat and consider how I fit into this man's worldview. For the remainder of our journey we ride in silence: the driver focused on the road, and me searching the passing landscapes through the window. I'll never find anything because I don't know what I am looking for, but I continue to search.

Why do people spend so much money on wrist watches? I ponder the question as I look at my reflection in the passenger window. Maybe a seven-hundred dollar watch does a better job of telling time than a cheap one. If time is money, then an expensive watch must provide more time. A high-end watch might even be comprised of a new age metal that rejuvenates your life force, providing the wearer a sense of vitality. The more likely answer is that vanity has made man spend too much on wrist watches. After all, what self-respecting man would be caught keeping track of time with a device priced at twenty-five dollars. I will forever be at ease knowing that mankind will be able to tell time in three different time zones and under one thousand metres of water from the wrist.

"Twelve fifty." The driver doesn't even look back at me. Here I always thought passengers looked down on the driver, but tonight the driver is looking down on me. On everyone.

"Keep the change." I casually give the driver a twenty. Regardless of the insult it might cause, my guilt has motivated me to leave a large tip. Fuck him, he can have it. I'm paying him off and I'm paying my conscious off so I can think about something else. My tip money is my indulgence. I slam the taxi door behind me and quickly put the experience behind me, my grand entrance into the pub is more important to me right now. Like in a Western, I can't help but picture myself casually pushing the pub door open with one hand. The door seems to float open as I stand stoically, head hanging low, one thumb hooked into the belt loop of my pants, and my free arm swinging wildly as I strut into the bar. Every head turns and every conversation comes to an abrupt pause as they catch a glimpse of the mysterious silhouette filling the doorway. With all eyes fixated on me, I walk slowly towards the bar, each footstep carefully orchestrated so that my heel slaps the ground with a sharp sound, followed by a slide of my foot from heel to toe in an exaggerated gliding motion. The patrons of the pub slowly return to conversation, but never fully recover from the awe of my entrance. Women are enamoured by my rugged good looks and dishevelled appearance. In a Western there is something appealing about a loner with anger issues, but in real life an angry loner is not the apple of anyone's eye.

My real entrance to the bar bears little resemblance to the scenario I just played out in my imagination. I casually push the pub door open with one hand, but I only manage to open the door a quarter of the way. I try my best to slip through the small space I've opened up for myself, but I am suddenly pinned between the impossibly heavy door and its frame. Instead of pushing the door off myself, I just continue squeezing my body awkwardly through the tight space. Not a single person in the bar is affected by my entrance, every conversation continues to flourish, and not a single girl is enamoured by any aesthetic I have to offer. My stride does not exude confidence and would not qualify as stylish. The way my heel strikes the ground looks more like the march of a British soldier than the trot of a suave cowboy. I am strutting like I am angry at the ground, but the ground has caused me no offence. It suddenly occurs to me that the reason I have had so much antipathy towards exerting effort to look cool is that I am not cool. Nothing about me is smooth, polished, or enviable. I could give all the effort I have to give and I still wouldn't look cool.

I finally make my way to the bar, prop both my arms onto the counter, and position myself into a comfortable lean without drawing so much as a glance from anyone around me. I suppose that is a good thing, considering the show I just put on. Leaning against the bar I order a beer and begin surveying the room for Jeff. By now he's likely baited some girl into a reciprocal bout of flirting. Flirting is similar to small talk, but much more suggestive. Each player uses their eyebrows and playful exchanges of contact to make the words they say seem more meaningful. At some point both players will notice that they are making advances on each other and will position their defence to make it as easy as possible for the other person to score on them. Do couples flirt?

The bartender presents me with a beer and mouths something. He's likely telling me how much I owe, but he's much too soft-spoken to be heard over the pulsing bass of the music. I pull a ten out of my pocket and put it on the table, and then look up at the bartender to see if he is satisfied by the ten-dollar bill I've just placed in front of him. The bartender pockets the ten into his apron and moves on to another customer. Either he is assuming I am leaving a tip or I just bought a ten-dollar drink. Taking my beer, I am surprised by a hand grabbing my shoulder and pulling me back abruptly.

"Well, look who strolled in." Jeff whips me gently in the stomach with the back of his hand. I hope this isn't some form of flirting. "I bet you think no one saw you get stuck in the doorway there, but don't worry. We saw it. Guess you haven't opened many doors since you've been off work. Forget how they operate?"

"I was hoping I got away with that one."

"If I were you, I would have hoped I got away with that seizure of a first few steps you took. You squeezing a pickle between those cheeks?" Jeff leans back, squinting his eyes at my butt.

"If I did, would you really want to know?"

Jeff thinks for a few seconds before replying, "Absolutely. I want in on whatever's in your butt."

Two girls beside us look over at Jeff and shoot him a quick glance of disgust before turning away from us. Rather than allowing the two girls to retreat back into their own conversation, Jeff confronts them with a smile and shouts, "Hi ladies. You seem interested in our conversation, care to join us?" The two girls laugh and turn their bodies away from us. "Your loss." Jeff walks away from the bar, still beaming with confidence. I follow, assuming he is leading me to where Steve and Mary are seated. We arrive at a corner table located in a poorly lit section of the pub. Steve and Mary are deep into a conversation and don't even notice our arrival until we sit down.

"I don't believe you," Mary says. Her words may express disbelief, but her tone clearly indicates that she believes whatever it is Steve just told her. "So Reid had no idea, and just kept presenting?"

"Well, either he didn't know, or he didn't care." Steve laughs, looks over at me, and continues, "So, can you believe it? Reid was doing one of his staff pep talks today…"

"Not much pep in it," Mary interrupts.

"So he's giving one of his usual talks in the staff boardroom. He's just pointing away at the PowerPoint behind him, walking up and down the room, getting real close to everyone. The whole time he has the biggest pee dot on his pants. Guess he's too busy to give a good shake."

"I'm pretty sure the dot touched me. I felt the dampness on my forearm," Jeff says with a straight face.

Lifting up her glass to take a drink, Mary quips, "I'd be more concerned with him pressing something else up against your arm."

Mary's just one of the guys, drinking beers, swapping stories, and never talking about feelings. I'm also noticing for the first time just how similar Steve and Jeff are. They have the same neatly trimmed, brushed to the side haircut. They share the same affable mannerisms. Both Jeff and Steve manage to make me feel envious of how cool and together they are. They have a way of always being able to fit in and they are always well-liked. Neither Jeff nor Steve ever show any sign of stress or concern for the future and they always manage to stay current with the most popular style of shirt. What surprises me the most is how neither Steve's or Jeff's shoes ever show any sign of wear and tear. The scuff marks typical of any regularly-worn shoe do not seem to form. Ever. Have they discovered a more careful way to walk? It's more likely that they spend their nights buffing in some sort of shoe care product. They might even buy new shoes every month, while I lack the awareness of my surroundings to notice the subtle change in their foot attire. My mind is completely focused on replaying every memory I have of Jeff and Steve just so I can focus on their footwear. In my contemplation, two new pieces of information come to my attention. One, I cannot seem to recall which memories should be of Jeff, and which memories should be of Steve. Jeff and Steve have become interchangeable in my recall. I'll stick with one memory and try to sort it out.

I'm at work. It's some sort of office party. I can't remember why, most likely just a holiday. Everyone's standing up near the staff lunchroom but I'm seated away from everyone at my desk. I'm suddenly startled by Jeff as he shouts, "Hey!" and leans into my cubicle. Or is it Steve. Steve leans into my cubicle and shouts.

Steve is now in my cubicle and he's brought a spare drink.

"Libations, free and during work hours. What kind of slave works through this opportunity?" Jeff is talking loudly enough that everyone around us can hear. He raises his voice and shouts,

"Eh, Dave?"

It's clear that statement is less directed at me than it is directed at Dave. Jeff starts laughing because he knows Dave the Slave is squirming behind his desk, working hard through the staff party because he doesn't know how to relax.

Now Steve is forcing a drink into my hand and doing his best to convince me to get out of my cubicle.

"Just have a few, only chance you'll get to drink on company time without getting shit canned."

I shake my head and end the memory sequence. It seems I can't distinguish who is Jeff and who is Steve. They just blend seamlessly into one person. The second piece of information that has come to my attention is that Jeff and Steve always seem to have perfectly ironed and tucked in dress shirts. I spend so much of my time during the workday trying to keep my shirt tucked in that this really bothers me. Every movement I make seems to work against my struggle to keep my professional image intact. Every shelf I reach up to, every time I move from a slouch into an upright-seated position, the cusp of my shirt always finds a way to break free of my pants.

Am I the only person who can't keep their shirt tucked in?

Steve and Jeff are fully-functioning adults. Life does not weigh them down and their shirts seem to be perfectly tailored to fit their every movement.

Sitting back into my chair, I take a few sips from my beer. Steve, Jeff, and Mary are still laughing and carrying on, but I find myself focusing more on the random people around me. The scene at the bar shares a striking resemblance to a recent documentary I viewed on the mating habits of apes. Examining the bar, I see men engaged in primal competition for the attention of females. Circling the dance floor, these men are beating their chests and flexing their muscles to win the admiration of nearby women. Nothing but emotive grunts are shared between the men vying for the attention of the most attractive women in the bar. After a few minutes of examining the dance floor, it becomes quite clear who has drawn the attention of all the women and now has an inescapable target on his back. Every male aggressively displaying his mating prowess must challenge the alpha to garner attention from the female patrons. I can see the cold stares from the males roaming the outskirts of the dance floor. As my gaze moves closer to the centre of the dance floor, I can see the first challenger for male dominance make his move. Incidental contact is made as the challenger's shoulder strikes the alpha male's shoulder, resulting in the spilling of a drink and a drawn out stare down. A verbal challenge is issued,

"The fuck you lookin' at?" The challenger postures by puffing out his chest and placing his hands down by his sides, but with a noticeable gap as if his lat muscles are too large to allow his hands to come to rest at his sides.

"You wanna go?" Words spoken loud enough by the challenger that every person in the bar can hear. If the challenge is met, a new alpha male may be established. A hush captivates the patrons of the bar as all eyes are on the challenge that has been issued. The tension in the room is palpable, but quickly dispelled by several bouncers. Bouncers are a wild card. They are not part of the natural order of the dance floor, and they exert an undue amount of power over all patrons. Ironically, despite their prowess, they are not sought after as ideal candidates for intercourse by the female patrons.

The bar is an irritating place for me to be. It is a constant reminder of how primitive we still are. Men and women still sniffing the air and presenting themselves in the hopes of attracting a suitable mate. The omegas are poised on the periphery of the dance floor, hoping that a female patron's ability to make an informed decision is impaired enough to allow for their courting attempts to succeed. Is it possible that someday we might evolve past this game? Sex becomes nothing but a mechanism to perpetuate the human race, and is done without emotion, attachment, or games. Suitable mating partners are established through careful examination of DNA and offspring are purposefully brought into existence. The late night bar scene might cease to exist, and the human race might start going to sleep early enough to be productive in the morning. Pregnancy might even spur new industry resulting from tight regulation surrounding the use of sperm and ovaries. Licenses to breed might be issued and periodically reviewed to ensure the human race trends in the right direction.

"So, sounds like Dave and Jason were laid off." Leaning back into her chair, Mary gives a moment for her news to sink in. I watch her gauging our responses. "I mean, it's still just a rumour. I heard it from Linda, she said she saw termination letters on Reid's desk. She swears that Dave and Jason's name are on two of them."

"How'd she *just happen* to see it?" Steve scoffs, clearly not believing in Linda's reconnaissance ability.

Jeff cuts Mary off before she has a chance to answer, panic dripping from his voice and body language. "Wait, wait. Back up a second. Did she see any other termination letters? Any other names? I mean, is this a big layoff?

"She didn't say." Mary straightens her posture and trying to project confidence. "It doesn't feel like that's the direction it's heading. I mean, normally there'd be some sort of HR review of all our jobs. Y'know, where every fifteen minutes we have to write down every stupid thing we do."

Jeff laughs, "Last time we did that, I made sure to tell them what I did every bathroom break." With a deep sigh that betrays Jeff's normally unflappable demeanor, he directs the spotlight towards me. "You've been pretty quiet for a while. What do you think?"

"About Dave? I guess I'm wondering, who will take his place."

Mary jumps in "I doubt they hire anyone new. Honestly, Jeff is probably right about more people being laid off soon. We'd probably all be better off if we started looking for new jobs, I mean look at everything that's been happening lately."

Maybe Dave's unfortunate circumstance is the push I need to force myself into a new environment where I have to grow into someone different. "Could be good for us to look around for new jobs. But that's not entirely what I meant. I'm wondering who will become the next Dave the Slave. You know, someone that gets dumped on. There's always someone filling that role."

Steve throws some napkins at me and laughs. "What, worried it's going to be you? I would be after the scene you put on the other week. You might need a new job to get away from that."

Laughing, I find myself smiling and throwing the napkins back at Steve. "What are you saying, you want me to leave?" I'm almost enjoying myself right now. I'm reciprocating the light hearted smiles and banter of Steve, Mary, and Jeff.

Our jovial mood is brought to an abrupt halt by Mary's sobering admission. "To be honest with you guys. I've been looking around and applying for other jobs. Nothing yet, but it's only a matter of time."

Looking down at his drink, Jeff's voice almost seems as if it's been slowed down. "That kind of bums me out to be honest. That whole place is really going down hill ... I'm starting to think we might all be on our way out." Jeff looks up from his drink and takes a second to look us all in the eye. "Nothing really seems certain anymore, does it."

Silence takes hold as we all exchange awkward glances and nods of the head. I've been so blind to the misery of my company.

Steve breaks the silence. He is uncomfortable and looking to escape what has quickly become an uncomfortable conversation.

"Well, I've got a few in me. I'm going to try my luck on the dance floor. See if I can put out some vibes." Standing up, Steve shoots us a wink that seems to say, *whatever happens I'm not going to let it get me down,* then makes his way to the dance floor.

"So when are you back at work?" Jeff leans forward on the table.

"Well, my two weeks are pretty much up. To be honest, I sort of expected some sort of phone call or email from Reid by now, telling me to be back for Monday. So I guess I'll just stroll in, see what happens."

"Oh man, what I wouldn't give for two weeks off. I mean, besides the two weeks they so graciously give us for vacation every year."

"You know, Jeff, I never really pegged you as a guy that hated work."

"You kidding? Who doesn't hate work. It's just something you gotta get through, you know? Wouldn't mind sleeping in more often." Jeff picks up his beer and looks towards the dance floor listlessly.

I guess I'm not so different from Jeff after all.

"Growing up wasn't quite what I pictured it would be when I was a kid." I take a drink from my beer, joining Jeff in gazing out towards the dance floor.

"When I was a kid, I always thought I'd grow up to be a firefighter. Then I learned firefighters scrape dead people from car seats, so I sort of just ended up in this gig for lack of imagination. Could be worse, I guess." Jeff puts his beer down and turns towards me. "Whaddaya say we round up Steve and Mary, grab a shot. Talk about something else, eh?"

"Where is Mary? Didn't notice her take off."

"Yah, you really should try to notice her a little more. You know, she did like you. Now she's out there dancing with some goof in a v-neck shirt that's cut way too low. Probably waxes his chest too."

I can't help but laugh. "You know, Jeff, I never thought you could be so bitter. I don't mind this side of you."

I'm laughing. I'm smiling. Who is this person that's suddenly taken control, is he planning on staying? Maybe if I ask politely he will take up residency.

Chapter 31

It's Monday morning and my mandated two weeks of time away from work have drawn to a close. I respond instinctively to my alarm clock, like some machine programmed to perform a mundane task. Normally, I would feel uneasy about having to go to work all day, but this morning a slight change to the routine seems to have pulled me in a different direction. A small pill I swallowed before eating cereal has sparked thoughts of Steve, Jeff, and Mary. Maybe they aren't so bad. I found myself wanting to spend time with them this weekend, and I surprised myself by having fun. It took a while to let go of the tension I've been carrying around with me for years. Tension that *I let go*. It feels good to exert control over something in my life. I'm not a marionette strung along by some deranged artist making a statement about futility. I am the deranged artist.

To demonstrate my newfound artistry, I shake up the morning routine in a very subtle, post-modern way. I brush my teeth before showering, put my socks on before my underwear, and stop buttoning my shirt one short of the top. I don't want to feel like I'm being strangled by a pair of weak hands; I want to breathe and experience full range of motion. No tie. Just comfort and an open collar. Staring at myself in the mirror, I take a deep breath and then exhale. Time to saddle up and drive to work.

On the way to my car I walk past a dog sitting on a patch of grass outside the front of the apartment. Wagging his tail side to side he seems to be taking in all the events unfolding in the parking lot, watching everyone walk to their cars, following birds as they take off from the ground, and tracking all the squirrels climbing around the trees. Is it possible to be as happy as a dog? Here he is, just sitting and soaking in the world. Is he thinking anything, or just watching? What would that even be like, to be totally in the moment and experiencing life unravel second by second without worry for the future or confusion about the present? Turning my head, I glance up at the sunrise and the brilliant display of colour saturating the clouds in the sky. I'm going to follow the example of this dog and just stare at the sky for a minute. No thoughts. My lips curl upward into what is unmistakably a smile as I gaze.

Inhale. Exhale. Freedom from thought.

My trance is eventually broken by the jarring scream of a jackhammer, but for a moment I could feel what this dog feels, relaxed and happy to be outside and part of the world. I didn't feel the pressure of having to play a role – I didn't feel at all. I found myself lost in the skyline. Glancing over at the dog, I give a quick nod and then depart for my car. This dog may not be aware of the moment we just shared, but I felt I should acknowledge anyway.

Pulling into the parking lot at work I decide that today is going to be the day I follow the crowd and use the front door to walk into the office. I don't usually walk through the front door, so at first I am not put off by the large crowd standing to one side of the door. I also don't seem to be put off by the cop cars just to the left of the crowd. Something clearly isn't right here. I can see Jeff leaning coyly against the far side of the building by himself. He usually arrives at work early, so he must know what's going on. Making my way towards Jeff, I shoot him a gesture that best represents my curiosity by raising my shoulders and scrunching my mouth.

"I don't even think you'll believe it."

I lean up against the wall beside Jeff. "So what happened? Reid arrest someone for stealing pens?"

"No, it's Dave."

"The Slave?"

"Yah, Dave the Slave. So picture this. Some girl spots Dave sitting in his car this morning, just screaming and slamming his fists on his wheel. Total meltdown and there's no one else in the car, so she thinks to herself *this guy must be just losing his mind.* She freaks out and notifies security. So Dave probably spends about another ten minutes in the car, having an absolute breakdown. Someone else walks by and sees him packing something suspicious into a bag. Looks like a weapon, so this person freaks out and notifies security too.

"Now security has two strange reports about the same guy, so they send a security officer down to the entrance and notify the police. I mean, they're only security guards, right? They're trained to check your ID at the door and make sure you sign in. Anyway, so Dave gets out of his car and walks towards the entrance. The security guard sees Dave holding a large bag that looks heavy, so the guard panics a bit. As Dave approaches the guard, the guard yells out for him to stop, but Dave just keeps walking. So the guard steps in between the door to block Dave's path. He tells Dave that *he's had two reports of erratic behaviour and a potential report of a weapon.* Tells him that he's *going to need to see what's in the bag.* Well, I can only imagine a standoff ensued, and Dave just said, *sure, I'll show you what's in the bag.* The crazy fuck pulls out a gun; the security guard panics and tries to tackle him. Dave manages to fire off a shot before the guard grabs him. He gets a few more shots off but the guard manages to wrestle Dave to the ground and pin his arm down. The other guard runs over and helps make sure he's restrained, somewhat uncomfortably with a knee in his back. During all of this, people come running from all over the parking lot to see what the hell is happening, which is weird because, I mean a gun just went off … I'm pretty sure I'd take off in the opposite direction. So anyway, crowd comes running up, Dave is held down by two security guards, one is bleeding from his shoulder, there is an open bag with a few guns visible in it just to the side of them, and cops come screeching into the parking lot. Good thing they made the call, right? So the cops come out, arrest Dave, and an ambulance arrives shortly after to take the security guard away. There are a few cops left here now taking statements, trying to make sure they got the whole story."

"Dave? Are you fucking kidding me? He brought guns to work? How'd you find all this out?"

"I heard it from Nancy. Apparently she talked to whoever made the second report to the police. She was also one of the people who ran over and saw the end of the wrestling match go down."

Both Jeff and I remain leaning against the wall, looking on the crowd of people in silence. The note I received two weeks ago, the note that caused me to go into counselling, was from Dave. He really did plan to kill me last, which makes me wonder why no one else said anything about a little yellow note. Was I the only one who got it? Or was I the only one who noticed.

"Did you ever get a note?"

With his focus locked onto the crowd, Jeff lazily addresses my question. "Note?"

"Yellow post-it note. Threat on it?"

"Threat?" Jeff shakes his head. "Should I have?"

"Never mind," I say. "Forget it."

"I guess this means we might get the day off work then, huh." Jeff turns towards me and smiles.

"Jeff, there's something I've been wondering." I put my hands in my pockets and keep staring at the ground. The difficult question makes eye contact uncomfortable. "Why is it you always go out of your way to talk to me?"

Jeff laughs but doesn't answer my question. He crosses his arms and looks over at me briefly before joining me in looking at the ground.

"Really, though. I mean, what's the difference between Dave and I? It's not like I ever really went out of my way to be a friendly person. What makes me worth all the time and effort?"

"Well, you weren't always such a space cadet. When we first started here, you were pretty decent to be around. Kind of reminded me of my brother. I started to get a little worried about you though. You stopped laughing, stopped smiling. You sort of faded away. So I figured I oughtta cheer up an awful bastard like you."

"What about Dave?"

"What about him?"

"Was he not worth cheering up?"

"You look like you hated being at work. Dave looked like he loved being at work and I can't really relate to someone liking work that much. I guess I thought he was screwy in the head maybe. I always knew there was a reason

I avoided working hard." Jeff sighs and looks over at me. "Why do you ask? Is all this making you, I don't know … start questioning? You know?"

"All this?" I ask.

"Yah, all this. Sudden brush with death. Had Dave made it in, we might be dead around now. It hit me pretty hard, to be honest. Before you came over I was over here feeling sick to my stomach. I started thinking about everything. If I suddenly stopped being alive, would I be OK with that? I mean, I'd be dead – so I guess I wouldn't have a choice."

Taking a deep breath, I look up to the sky and exhale slowly. "I think I've been caught up in that for a while now. The past few years have been a struggle."

Jokingly, Jeff tries to break the tension. "What, was spending time with us that bad? You were no ray of sunshine either, you know."

"No, I suppose not." I smile. "I think one day I just wondered, what the hell is the point you know." Looking around, I throw my arms up. "What is the point of all this? What am I doing? If I died today, and in my last breath I had to defend what all of it had been about, I'd have nothing to say. I'd just shrug."

"Maybe there is no point. Live for today, and all that."

I laugh and ask, "How do you do it, Jeff? You always seem to be happy. Work doesn't bring you down. You go out, enjoy yourself, people enjoy being around you. Life isn't a grind for you."

"Well," Jeff takes a long pause, "I guess I've never really thought about that. If I'm on the spot here, I'd have to say I just keep it simple."

"Simple?"

Jeff shrugs. "Simple. Don't make it out to be a grind. Make it out to be something else."

"That's it?"

"Yes." Jeff looks me in the eye. "That's it."

"Aren't you oversimplifying?"

Jeff pushes himself off the wall and laughs. "You sound jealous."

I watch Jeff walk into the crowd of onlookers, bright red tones flickering off everyone's skin from the police lights. It all seems so surreal. Are they looking on with guilt, or are they firm in believing Dave is just crazy? What will the evening news sound bites sound like? *We never saw it coming. Dave was so quiet and polite.* I'm sure we will all conveniently forget how we bullied him relentlessly by isolating him, and justifying it by blaming his own behaviour.

Maybe if I wasn't so absorbed in my own problems, I could have … I don't know, done something. Cared more? I knew what was going on. I could see it. Feel it. Yet I just let everything unfold, choosing to brood on my own problems instead of helping Dave. I might as well have given him a gun.

I used to think I was the only person who hated waking up. Hated the way I had let life turn out. I guess we are all just going through the motions, struggling to let ourselves find anything to be happy about in a sea of excuses and blame. Inside all of us there is an internal struggle to accept what we have to give up in order to get by in the world. Fantasy is replaced by pragmatism. Dreams are exchanged for S.M.A.R.T. goals. Freedom is tempered by responsibility. One day you realize your future is here and you're not who you want to be. You're never going to be where you want to be. You could change direction now, but fear dissuades you.

Fear that all those years you spent heading in the wrong direction were meaningless.
Fear that you may fail.
Fear that you may never find a sense of purpose.

Fear grips us and meaning eludes us because we made it all up. We made up the word *meaning*, and we made up the concept of *purpose*.

We made up everything.

Humans had to go and create language, hence birthing a ceaseless age of defining, explaining, and comparing. We will never be satisfied until we realize our own thoughts defined our expectations for life, explained our disappointment in the outcome, and compared our outcome to that of others.

Life is a series of anecdotes about the burden of consciousness that we won't get to tell until we've gained enough perspective to unravel the layers of the lesson and take it to heart. I'm starting to unravel and take to heart my complicity in my misery.

Work didn't make me sad.

The people around me didn't make me miserable.

No one forced me to be an asshole.

Medication didn't turn my life around. Neither did Tim. Medication and therapy helped me realize I am and always have been the wizard behind the curtain of everything I feel. I can choose to keep it simple and not make it out to be a grind. If I take down the curtain, I'm just another flawed, confused, and anxious person using my misconceived lack of heart, brains, and courage as an excuse for all my failings.

Watching cops move from person to person, I can't help but think of Dave and everything he went through. Maybe it's not enough to just focus inward on the man behind the curtain. Maybe the wizard ought to focus on the impact he has on Oz and the people in it. Is that the secret to happiness and living in the moment, embracing the inexorable relationship between myself and the people around me? Choosing to live *with* the world as opposed to living *aside* the world?

Now I just have to figure out how to do that.

Afterword:

Everyone struggles, few talk about it. This story has been written to contribute to the dialogue on mental health and well-being. This is a topic that impacts our ability to participate and enjoy life.

The dialogue continues below with words from family, friends, and colleagues who contributed to the publication of this story

"Three things help me. First, to remember that happiness
is a state of mind, not an end in itself. It will come and go,
as do other emotions and states. I can't be happy all the time,
just as I can't sleep or work or be creative all the time.
Second, to seek it in small doses and let it recharge my
batteries for the days when I really need to draw on
that reserve. And third, my level of happiness is directly
proportional to my level of gratitude."
– *Hanusia Tkaczyk*

"The pursuit of happiness starts within yourself.
Don't go anywhere till you have looked there first."
– *Lynn Wood*

"For those struggling with mental illness or caring for someone
who does, it can be very isolating, overwhelming, and at times
painful. We need to listen, share, and support those who are
suffering. Together, WE can all make a difference. Mental
illness can touch us all. It does not discriminate – why do we?"
– *Kathy Nizol*

"Mental health can kill someone just like cancer or another illness. Combined with addiction, or addiction as a function of mental health, it can be deadly. I lost a close friend of mine due to mental health and addiction issues in December 2015. He took his own life. If he had not been passed over by the health system, or just dismissed as a drug addict, or some silly kid, perhaps he would still be with us. I'd like to take this opportunity to publicly remember my friend, Rhett Cappleman, and state that his death was not in vain. His death has gotten me to speak out and be more aware of and compassionate toward mental health and addiction problems.

"If you feel something isn't quite right, talk to someone ... a friend, your doctor, parent, teacher, relative, cousin, professor ... because there is no shame in asking for help.
It takes a damn strong person to reach out and ask for help to pull themselves through something and make changes.
Take pride in that if you feel you need some help and ask for it.
You cannot do it on your own – trust me."
– *Lindsay Grad*

"Even in our sleep
pain which cannot forget
falls drop by drop upon the heart
Until in our own despair
Against our will
Comes wisdom"
– *Aeschylus*

Poem shared by Judy Grad

61608329R00120

Made in the USA
Middletown, DE
13 January 2018